Glimmer Vale

Glimmer Vale Chronicles, #1

Michael Kingswood

Glimmer Vale

Glimmer Vale Chronicles, #1

Michael Kingswood

Additional Works

Acknowledgements

Many thanks to the people who assisted in creating this book: Jim Beveridge and Cindie Geddis from Lucky Bat Books, who supplied the wonderful cover art, Jared Blando, who created the interior artwork and map, and Ryan Smith, Jan Thomas, and Mark Fassett, who provided editorial and proofreading support.

Table Of Contents

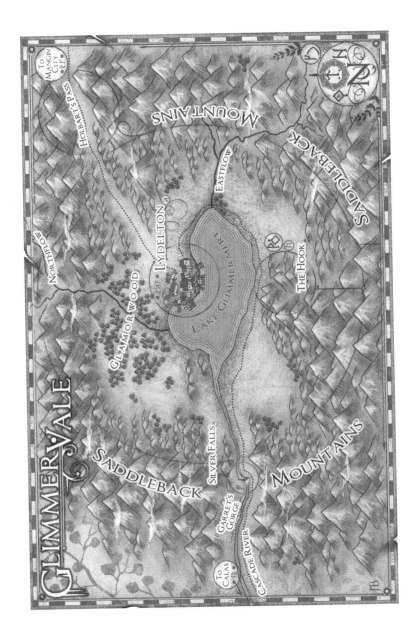

Chapter One

Garret's Gorge

Cold wind whipped past Julian, making his cloak furl out behind him. Biting back a curse, he clutched at the flapping cloth and pulled it back in tight around his body, but not before the momentary exposure had done its damage. What small warmth he had been able to retain was gone, leaving him to shiver in his saddle. The mail shirt he wore didn't help matters, but he had learned the hard way not to go without it.

It was supposed to be getting on into Spring. Down below, in the lowlands many miles behind him, farmers were tilling their fields in preparation for the first planting. Trees and bushes were beginning to show their first buds. And people could go about their business in less than three layers of clothing. But not here, among the peaks of the Saddleback Mountains. Here, winter still clung to the land like a young maiden with her first crush.

"Tell me again why we're taking this route?" he muttered with annoyance.

Julian's companion looked sidelong at him and rolled his

eyes. Raedrick was a hand taller than Julian and thin as a stick, with shoulder-length black hair that was tied into a short ponytail at the nape of his neck. Like Julian, Raedrick wore a cowled brown cloak of thick wool over his mail, and calf-high leather riding boots. Beyond that their fashion sense deviated, for while Raedrick usually picked shirts and pants of blue and grey, Julian preferred greens and browns; they went with his short brown hair and hazel eyes better.

Or at least that's what the ladies told him.

When they first met, Julian thought sure he could break Raedrick in half with one hand. He had quickly learned the folly of that. Raedrick was quick, and a lot stronger than he looked. And he could wield the saber that hung from his saddle horn with deadly efficiency.

"I don't feel like getting caught, do you?" Raedrick said. "Not many people come this way anymore since the southern passes became viable. Plus, it's faster."

"I'd almost rather take my chances down south," Julian replied.

It had been a hard week since they departed Calas. The army did not generally chase deserters, but all the same if a chance patrol happened upon them, they were done. So they took pains to remain out of sight, which meant they mostly traveled at night.

That had been bad enough, but once they made it into the foothills of the mountains, past even the most distant picket lines, the journey had gotten steadily worse. At first Julian had thought riding in the day again would be easier, but as the terrain became more rugged their progress slowed and the day's ride grew more exhausting.

Then, the day before yesterday, they passed through the last of the trees and emerged onto the bare flank of the mountains, leaving them completely exposed to the elements.

Fierce gusting winds and lowering temperatures conspired to create a thoroughly miserable day and a restless night. They finally got a bit of relief yesterday afternoon as they put the first few peaks behind them, and then again this morning when they entered Garret's Gorge. But that was a respite only compared to the bitter cold of the mountain range's flanks, as the last wind gust revealed.

At least they had a nice view. Julian had to concede that.

About ten feet to his left, the road abruptly fell away. A sheer cliff, and another one a tenth of a mile away facing it, formed the walls of the Gorge. At the bottom, a couple hundred feet down, the Cascade River flowed, a long series of rapids that only subsided in the foothills far to the west, where it merged with the River Lonaylay on its way to the Tymor Sea. Between the Gorge and the mighty peaks all around, there was always another awe-inspiring sight here. But right then Julian would trade it all for a nice fire and a warm mug of mulled wine. And a warmer maiden.

"Quit complaining," the other man said. "We're almost to the falls. From there it's just barely a half day to Lydelton."

Julian only grunted in reply.

They rode in silence for another hour. Slowly, almost imperceptibly, a low noise began to intrude on Julian's consciousness. At first it was easy to not notice it, a low rumble that could just as easily be his imagination. But the rumble grew over time until eventually it became impossible to ignore.

"What's that? The falls?"

Raedrick nodded with a wry grin. "Just around the next corner. Brace yourself."

Julian snorted. He had seen plenty of waterfalls before. One was much the same as... They rounded the corner and Julian abandoned the thought as his jaw dropped in amazement.

The falls were about a quarter of a mile ahead. Spilling over the side of a jagged mountain peak that rose high above all the others nearby, the falls had to have measured a thousand feet from the dropoff to the bottom of the Gorge, where the river began to flow. Mist billowed off the water as it fell and rose in a great cloud at the falls' base. The rocks on either side of the Gorge and on the adjoining flank of the mountain gleamed, frozen mist reflecting the mid-morning sunlight that shined from the west. Julian instantly understood why they were called Silver Falls; if he didn't know better, he would have thought the ice was precious metal from the way it reflected the sunlight.

"Gods be good," he said. Or at least, he tried to say it. Even at that distance, the roar from the falls was tremendous. He could barely hear himself speak.

"We'll need to protect our ears as we get closer." Raedrick leaned over close to Julian's ear as he spoke. Even still, it was hard to understand him.

Julian nodded and flipped open one of his saddlebags. After a moment of digging, he found a small lump of wax. Breaking it in two, he held the two pieces in his fists for a moment to soften them up. Then he pressed them into his ears. The roar was immediately muffled, though it was still distinctly noticeable.

The two men continued forward. The great mountain peak rose on their side of the Gorge, blocking their path like a colossus. But the road shortly veered away from the Gorge and the peak itself, instead climbing the mountain's flank on the other side of the peak from the falls. Julian considered, as they turned on the first of what would probably be many switchbacks designed to lessen the road's angle of ascent, that it was probably for the best. He didn't want to think about how difficult the road would be to follow if it was covered in ice from the mist. So the extra few miles to go around the peak were probably worthwhile.

Just before noon, after more switchbacks than Julian wanted to count, they reached the road's highest point and paused for a moment. Looking down from their lofty perch, Julian was struck by the beauty of the valley before them.

The road descended across the face of the mountain and made its way back to the river just above the falls, then followed the river to a large lake shaped like a kidney bean that dominated the center of the valley: Lake Glimmermere, if Julian remembered his maps correctly. Still except for the wakes from a number of boats making way around the lake, the water reflected the mountains on the other side of the valley with near-pristine clarity.

Off to the north of the lake, the valley was wooded all the way up into the mountains. To the south, a few copses punctuated the rolling hills, but for the most part there was only grassland except for a narrow spur of mountains that pushed north almost to the shore of the lake. Two rivers flowed into the lake: one from the north and one from the east. A number of what Julian assumed were farming hamlets clustered in the grasslands surrounding the eastern river. Almost directly opposite the two men on the other side of the valley, Holbart's Pass led away off to the northeast.

But the thing that truly drew Julian's eye was the fair-sized town on the north shore of the lake. A sprawling collection of buildings large and small surrounding a half-dozen piers that protruded into the lake like the fingers of some great grasping hand, the town of Lydelton might as well have been the most opulent metropolis in the world. Down there were warm Inns, home cooked meals, and wenches aplenty. He could hardly wait to get there.

"Glimmer Vale," Raedrick said in a soft tone. "I've not been here in years."

"Looks like a nice enough place."

Raedrick nodded. "The people are friendly and hospitable, and they have a local recipe for the fish from the lake that is to die for."

"Then what are we waiting for?" Julian spurred his horse to motion and began the descent. Behind him, he heard Raedrick chuckle before doing the same.

Going down was faster than coming up. Before long, they reached the base of the mountain. The road met the river a few hundred yards above the lip of the falls, near a small copse of evergreens. The river was narrow there, maybe a hundred feet across, but flowed swiftly toward the dropoff. Julian was struck by how much quieter it was here than down below. Oh, the falls' roar was still plain to hear, but it was nowhere near as deafening as it had been on the other side.

"I guess the Gorge makes it louder," he murmured to himself, earning a curious glance from Raedrick. Julian shrugged in response and gestured toward the falls.

Raedrick nodded. "A good thing, too. Can you imagine trying to live next to all that racket?"

Julian shuddered.

The road ran into the copse about twenty feet from the rocks overhanging the river. It was a pleasant change from the bare rock of the last couple days, and Julian found himself grinning as they passed beneath the trees' canopy. The smell of pine was soothing, reminding him of pleasant days from his past. He lost himself in enjoyment for a moment.

Which made the harsh voice that barked out at them all the more unpleasant.

"That's far enough. Stop right there."

Julian shook himself back to attention and groaned. Half a dozen men stepped out from behind the trees lining the road ahead. They were unshaven, wearing dirty cloaks and leggings that had seen better days. But they also had on what looked like high-quality leather breastplates that were lined with iron studs, leather gauntlets and bracers, and greaves on their shins. Five of them arranged themselves in a loose arc in the road ahead, while the sixth stood a few feet back and, nocking an arrow to his bowstring, drew back and sighted in on them.

Brigands.

Julian and Raedrick reined in their horses, and a burly man with a vicious-looking scar on his chin who stood in the center of the ring of five spoke. From his voice, he was the same man who spoke before. That made him the leader. "Your money or your life, boys," he said.

Nice welcome.

Chapter Two

A Warm Welcome

J ulian and Raedrick shared a brief look. This was annoyance they did not need. Julian raised one eyebrow and began inching his hand down toward the pommel of his sword, which hung in its baldric from his saddle horn, a far more comfortable place to keep it while riding than on his hip. Plus, it was easier to draw from there.

Raedrick saw the movement and gave a slight shake of his head. He always wanted to try to talk first. Of course, considering the numbers in this particular encounter, Julian couldn't really blame him much. He pulled his hand back and looked back at the brigands, waiting for Raedrick to take the lead.

"We don't have much money," Raedrick said.

A loud snort was the brigand leader's initial reply. "And yer gonna have a lot less. Hand it over!"

Raedrick sighed and looked back at Julian again. With a shrug, he said, "Alright. Hand it over, Julian."

Julian wore a small pouch tied to his belt. Moving very slowly, he untied it and held it up for the brigands to see. It was filled to overflowing. The leader's expression changed to one of satisfaction. The fellow to his right, wearing an expression of open greed, stepped forward and reached out for it.

"Here you are," Julian said and moved to toss it to the fellow. He breathed a curse as he apparently lost his grip earlier than he planned and, instead of landing in the brigand's hand, the pouch flopped onto the ground near Julian's horse's feet. "Sorry about that." He managed a sheepish grin.

The brigand bounded forward and bent over to collect the pouch at the same time as his leader shouted, "No, you idiot!"

The brigand stood back up, Julian's pouch in his hand, and looked back at the leader for a heartbeat. That was the opening Julian was looking for. He kicked with his left foot, catching the brigand square in the face as he was returning his gaze back to Julian.

With a crunch of breaking bone, the brigand went down, clutching at his nose and jaw.

There was a moment's shocked pause while the other brigands looked wild-eyed at their comrade. Julian drove his heels into his horse's side, urging him into a run. The gelding bounded forward, but only made it a few feet. A second brigand, more quick to recover than the others, grabbed at the horse's bridle and pulled for all he was worth. The world lurched beneath Julian as the horse stumbled and then began to fall.

He cursed again as he launched himself out of the saddle and off to the side. Tucking his shoulder as he hit the ground, Julian rolled to his feet and drew his belt knife. Then he spun around.

Raedrick was on his feet, laying about with his saber. The

brigand Julian had kicked was still down. Another had fallen beneath Raedrick's blade, and the brigand he faced wore an expression of panic as he parried, then ducked, then leapt backwards away from Raedrick's relentlessly fluid assault. Julian almost felt sorry for the man, having been on the receiving end of Raedrick's fencing prowess more than once in the sparring circle. Almost.

The archer was nowhere to be seen, though a single arrow was buried deep into a tree trunk not far from where Julian stood. Hopefully Raedrick had taken him out, or they were in trouble. But Julian didn't have the time to look around for him, as the brigand who grabbed his gelding was charging at him, followed by the brigand leader.

Julian adjusted his grip on the knife and settled into a loose, ready stance. He forced down a surge of fear as his fighter's mind calculated the odds of survival for a man who brought a knife to a sword fight. They were not good, in his experience.

Then the brigand reached him and, drawing his arm back, attacked with a powerful cut from Julian's left to right. It probably would have spilled his guts, but Julian bounded forward inside the brigand's swing. The brigand's sword arm struck Julian in the ribs and he wrapped his left arm around it, pinning it in place. At the same time, Julian stabbed upward with his knife. The brigand wore an expression of disbelief as the blade entered his neck, severing his carotid artery and trachea. Julian withdrew the knife and the brigand fell to the ground, spasming out the last of his life.

Ten feet away, the brigand leader came up short, his expression suddenly a mix of wariness and eager anticipation. Behind him, Raedrick was nowhere to be seen, though Julian heard the noise of more fighting somewhere off to the left.

The brigand leader smiled, his grin causing the puckered

scar on his chin to expand. For a second, Julian thought sure it was going to swallow the other man's face whole, it grew so large.

"This could be fun," Scarface said. "Pick up the sword." His voice was steady and calm despite the grin of excitement on his face. He gestured with his sword point toward his comrade's weapon, now lying at Julian's feet.

What was this? Either Scarface was very confident or very stupid. Or maybe both. But Julian wasn't about to question the sudden generosity. Slowly he lowered into a crouch and, replacing the knife into its sheath, he took hold of the sword.

Scarface came on in a rush, his weapon singing through the air as it descended toward Julian's neck.

Desperately parrying upward, Julian flung himself away from the assault. The clang of steel striking steel was still in the air as he completed a full backward roll and rose to his feet. Just in time to meet a second attack from the brigand leader. Another quick retreat left the cut to whistle harmlessly through the air.

Julian tried to counterattack, but Scarface's assault was relentless and he found himself driven backward again. And again. The man was good!

Parry, dodge, retreat.

Julian gave up more ground, and found himself leaving the copse and treading on the bare rock near the riverbank. Bending his knees to avoid a high cut, he attempted a riposte.

Somehow Scarface's high cut became a descending parry that knocked the thrust aside. Then Julian found the wind driven from his lungs as the brigand leader spun around and drove the heel on his boot into Julian's lower ribs.

He tumbled to the ground, unable to breathe and awash with pain from his ribs. He felt as much as heard Scarface's blade descending toward him and forced himself to roll over and raise his own sword.

Steel met steel again as the force of the cut's momentum drove the two hilts together in the air above Julian's body.

For a moment, the two men looked at each other through the frame of their entwined blades. Finally able to draw a breath, Julian saw that Scarface had barely broken a sweat and was breathing normally. He smirked, a mocking twist of the lips that carried no small amount of disdain, and leaned in, driving the two blades slowly downward despite Julian pushing upwards with all his strength.

"Ready to die?" he asked.

Julian knew he wasn't going to be able to keep the sword from falling for much longer. Already his arms were shaking from the strain of resisting.

Julian abruptly stopped fighting it and rolled with the force of Scarface's push, driving the swords in the ground beside where he lay. At the same time he kicked upward and to the side, catching Scarface on his hip. Now it was the brigand leader's turn to tumble to the ground.

In the brief respite, Julian bounded to his feet and backed away, gingerly feeling at his ribs with his left hand. The brigand leader flipped to his feet easily and assumed a ready stance, his blade held loosely in both hands with the tip pointing at Julian's eyes. He inclined his head in salute for a moment, the mocking smirk gone from his face.

Then he attacked again, and again Julian was driven back.

He gave ground with each exchange and only avoided severe injury on one occasion because of the mail shirt he wore. All the same, he accumulated several small cuts where his parry or dodge wasn't quite fast enough.

Scarface remained untouched.

The roar of the falls was louder now. Between parries,

Julian glanced over his shoulder and was shocked to see that he had retreated almost all the way to the edge of the river, only twenty yards or so from the drop off.

The glance cost him. Julian barely hopped back from another attack, but still took a deep cut in his thigh. He was running out of time and space, and now his balance was off as his thigh protested every movement. Julian attempted another counter, a rising cut toward the brigand leader's armpit.

He found his eyes growing wide with surprise as Scarface executed a highly stylized, spiraling parry that ended with the tip of his sword hooking beneath Julian's hilt. A flick of Scarface's wrists pulled the sword from Julian's hand and left him with a deep cut in the meat of his thumb.

The sword clattered away somewhere off to the right. Stunned, Julian took a half-step back and raised his hands. This couldn't be happening! The brigand leader sneered and snapped off a quick salute with his sword. "Well fought," he said before he began to move forward.

Frantic, Julian retreated again. Wait. Raedrick, where was Raedrick! Julian looked back toward the copse, but there was still no sign of his friend.

Scarface swung at him, and Julian leaned far backwards to avoid a cut that would have taken his head off. All the same, he felt the tip of the sword cut a line across the bridge of his nose.

He stumbled back and suddenly found he had nowhere else to go as his heels reached the edge of the rocks overhanging the river. Pinwheeling his arms for a moment to regain his balance, Julian glanced down at the swirling, frigid water as it rushed to the lip of the falls. This was it. He never once imagined it would end this way.

He looked up again just as Scarface attacked with a

backhanded swing that was again headed for his head.

In desperation, Julian moved forward and raised his right arm. Scarface's wrist struck the bones of his forearm.

Julian cupped his hand over the brigand leader's wrist and drove his palm upwards toward the back of his elbow. The sharp CRACK of breaking bone preceded Scarface's scream of surprise and pain by a heartbeat. His hand spasmed open, dropping the sword at Julian's feet, and his eyes went wide with shock, then wider still with dread as Julian pivoted about his rear foot and, using the arm as a lever, hurled the brigand leader over the edge of the rocks.

His arms and legs flailed at the empty air for a second, then the brigand leader splashed into the river. He bobbed to the surface quickly, but just as quickly began to sink again. Heavy boots and armor made swimming difficult, Julian thought with a certain satisfaction. He watched as Scarface splashed with his one good arm, trying with all his might to avoid being pulled under.

"Help me!" Scarface cried, to whom Julian couldn't guess since he certainly had no intention of lending a hand.

The current swept the hapless man toward the drop off. His swimming attempts became more frantic as he looked with horror toward the approaching edge.

"Help! Please!" he screamed.

Then he reached the edge and dropped out of sight. His last long scream of despair carried over the falls' roar for a moment, but was quickly overwhelmed.

"Well fought," Julian said.

Chapter Three

Glimmer Vale

J ulian limped back to the ambush site and found Raedrick tying up the bandit Julian kicked at the beginning of the fray. He didn't have a scratch on him, naturally. As Julian approached, Raedrick looked up and, upon seeing his condition, winced.

"You look like hell."

"Feel like it, too," Julian said. "Where did you go?"

"This guy hightailed it. You looked like you had things under control, so I went after him."

"Don't do that again. I really could have used the help."

Raedrick gave him a long, searching look, then nodded. "Sorry."

Hobbling over to his horse, Julian fished through the saddlebags until he found his medical supplies. Consisting of a few rags for bandages and a needle and thread, it wasn't much, but it would be sufficient for this job. "My leg and thumb are going to need stitches before we move out," he said.

Raedrick did the stitching once he had the prisoner

secured. Getting stitched up was never a fun experience, but having to lie there without pants in the chilly air just made it worse. The cold numbed his leg a bit, so the stitching itself wasn't as unpleasant, but taken as a whole, Julian would have preferred to do the deed in warmth. Fortunately, Raedrick was a good hand with a needle, so before too long he finished stitching and wrapped both wounds in snug bandages. Julian got dressed again and took a few ginger steps. The stitches seemed to hold well, but he would have to take it easy for a few days.

They took a few minutes to search the dead brigands. Julian was not surprised to find they had little money on them. But their armor and weapons were of good quality and would probably fetch a decent price, so he and Raedrick strapped those items down on their horses as well as they could. Their saddlebags were already full, so it was a very awkward packing job, but it would do for a short journey.

"What are we going to do with him?" Julian said, nodding toward their prisoner. "I'd say tie him to a tree and leave him for scavengers."

The brigand's eyes widened and he shook his head vigorously, but before he could speak Raedrick beat him to it.

"No. There's a Constable in Lydelton. He'll see that justice is done properly."

Julian frowned. "That's still a long way."

"About four, maybe five hours."

"We'd better get moving then if we want to get there before dark."

Raedrick nodded. While Julian slowly pulled himself up onto his saddle, his friend fished a length of rope out of his bag and tied one end into a knot around the brigand's neck. The other end he brought back to Julian. "Do you want the duty?"

Julian grinned and accepted the rope. Removing his baldric, he looped the rope around his saddle horn, making several turns to ensure it was secure. Then he draped the baldric over the saddle horn again and looked back at the brigand. "Hope you are a good runner, friend." It was perhaps heartless, but Julian got a lot of satisfaction from the brigand's terrified expression.

They set off at a slow trot, just barely above a jog, but after a half hour or so Julian heard a thud behind them, and the brigand began screaming. Reining in to a walk, he turned around to find the fellow dragging on the ground behind his horse. Julian rolled his eyes and pulled his horse to a full stop.

"I figured he'd be in better shape," he quipped to Raedrick, who shrugged. In a louder voice, Julian called back to the brigand, "On your feet! You're slowing us down!"

The brigand slowly pushed himself upright. It took a while, but Julian figured it was probably difficult with his hands tied behind his back. Beyond that, he was a mess. The right side of his face was scraped and bruised, his clothing was torn in several locations, he had a big red welt around his neck where the rope dug in, and he was panting heavily. Served him right.

As soon as the brigand was up again, Julian spurred the horse forward, at a walk this time. It was slower, but he had no real desire to torture the brigand to death. Killing a man in a stand-up fight was one thing. Dragging him behind a horse? That crossed the line into senseless cruelty.

The road followed the south bank of the river as it made its way east toward the Lake. Though the terrain to their right was mostly rolling hills, the road was, for the most part, level and made for an easy passage. So despite only moving at a quick walk, they made good time.

As they traversed the valley, Julian was again struck by the picturesque nature of the place. Everywhere he looked was another amazing view. When Raedrick told him of his plan to take this route, he had at first scoffed. Lydelton was a flyspeck of a town in the middle of nowhere. Why would anyone want to visit, let alone live there? Now that he had seen the valley, though, he was beginning to understand how it could be appealing. If only it was warmer.

As advertised from their high vantage point on the flank of the mountain, this part of the valley was mostly rolling grasslands, punctuated every so often with the occasional copse, some large enough to almost be rightly called forests themselves. There was no habitation as yet, but plumes of smoke in the distance announced fires from chimneys or forges.

After a couple hours, they drew near to the spit of mountains they had seen from above. The road became more wandering, to avoid the worst of the hills, as the mountains drew nearer. Until finally there was nothing for it but to go nearly straight up one side of a hill and straight down the next. The mountains came almost to the river; the main peaks could not have been more than a mile to the south. But from this vantage point, Julian could see that the peaks, which thrust northward from the main range to the south, bent to the east for a while before turning south again.

"The local's call this area The Hook," Raedrick said, seeing Julian eyeing the mountains as they rode. "Supposedly if you look at a quality map of this part of the Vale, the line of peaks forms a hook that bends off to the east and makes its own little concealed valley within a valley."

"Impressive," Julian replied.

Past The Hook, the land slowly flattened again until, by the time they reached the southeast corner of the lake, the hills were mostly gone. There, they began to see the first farmsteads. A single farmhouse here, a small cluster there, at first they were few and far between, but as the afternoon wore on, they became more frequent. All as he would have expected.

Then, about an hour and a half before sunset, not far from a ford across the river that flowed down to the lake form the mountains to the east, they encountered a farm that had been burned out. It had happened several days earlier based on the lack of smoldering and the general state of the place, but it was clear that the burning was not an accident. The front door was cloven in two as though by an axe or sword. Peaking inside, the remains of a large table had distinctive cut marks, as did one chair that somehow escaped the fire and stood pristinely in the midst of the destruction.

But the confirmation came when they stopped, at Raedrick's urging, to investigate the ruins more closely. There, within the husk of the burned house, lay two charred bodies: one larger and one small. The larger body, the mother Julian presumed, was clutching the smaller body as though to shield it from the flames and smoke. He supposed the fact that two people perished didn't rule out an accident. Until they then found a man's corpse, beheaded with his hands tied behind his back, in a small ditch not far behind the house.

"Hopefully they killed him first," Raedrick said, his tone carrying the same revulsion that Julian felt. "Can you imagine if they'd made him listen to his wife and child screaming inside the house before finishing him?"

"Who would do this?" Julian asked aloud. He looked back at their prisoner and found him close-mouthed, unwilling to look even in the same general area as the bodies. "Do you know, friend?" Julian asked, tugging at the rope as he did so.

Julian tugged on the rope, and the brigand jerked and turned a baleful eye on him. "Not a clue," he replied in an oily tone that just screamed the man was lying.

"Oh you know alright," Julian said. "Friends of yours, weren't they? Did they brag about it?" Anger began to well up within him and he found his voice rising. "Or did you go along for the ride, to have a little fun? Did you enjoy it, you sick bastard?" He began walking his horse back toward the brigand as he spoke. The brigand's expression grew frightened, then terrified, as Julian approached.

"Enough, Julian. He'll get justice from the Constable," Raedrick growled as he spurred his horse in front of Julian. "Remember?"

Julian took a long, deep breath to get himself back under control. After a moment, he nodded to Raedrick and turned his horse away. "Then let's get moving. The sooner we dump this fellow off, the better."

Chapter Four

Lydelton

As they rode into Lydelton, Julian was surprised to find the road paved. He had expected dirt streets, or at best cobblestones, but the main street into the town was paved with what looked like squares of flagstone.

"How did this happen?" he asked Raedrick.

The other man shrugged. "There's a rock quarry a little ways up in the mountains east of here. Back before I first came here, some folks got the idea to use some of that rock to pave the streets. They only got the main street done before deciding it was too much effort, or something."

Julian chuckled.

But his humor faded quickly as he looked from the paving stones to the people in the town. A dozen, maybe twenty, townsfolk were walking the main street as their horses began clopping down the road. One and all turned toward the sound of the horses' hooves with expressions of dread. A woman nearby clutched her small child and pulled him close as though unwilling to let him come near them. The weight of all those fearful eyes was nerve racking.

"What gives? I thought you said these people were friendly?"

Raedrick shook his head slowly. "I've no idea." Turning his gaze toward a young man, barely old enough to need to shave more than every other day, who had stopped in the street not far from them, he nodded in greeting and smiled. "Hello there. Can you point us toward the Constable's office?"

The young man blinked and for a moment looked as though he was going to bolt. But then he looked from Raedrick's smile to the brigand trailing behind them, and the rope tied around his neck, and he swallowed then answered. "Three blocks down, then make a right. First building on the left." He paused for a moment as though unsure of himself, then spoke again. "You're not with...him...are you." Gesturing toward the bound brigand, his voice sounded almost hopeful.

Julian snorted.

"Him?" Raedrick replied. "He and a few others tried to rob us on the road here. We're taking him to the Constable for justice. His friends weren't so lucky."

The young man's eyes widened and a large grin spread across his face. Looking around, Julian could see the tension leave the other people on the street in a flood. As they spurred their horses forward and moved on down the street, the eyes continued to follow them, but the murmur of hushed discussions sprang up among the townsfolk as well. Julian caught the word "heroes" a few times. What was that all about?

They found the Constable's office right where the young

man said it was. Just off the main street, on a side street that was paved, if that was the right word for it, with assorted rocks and gravel, it was a small, functional place. Short stairs led to a porch and a wide set of double doors at the front of the building. A simple sign, reading "Constable", hung over the door.

"Looks like this is it," Raedrick quipped as he dismounted and tied his horse off on a hitching post in front of the building.

"You are a master of the obvious," Julian replied with a grin.

He made quick work tying his horse off. Then he grabbed his baldric from around his saddle horn and, donning it, walked over to the brigand. "Time to face the music, friend," he said as he untied the knot around the brigand's neck.

The rope dropped to the ground and for a second Julian thought the brigand was going to try to make a run for it, no matter how exhausted and beaten-down he was. But with his hands bound and the pair of them ready to chase him down he wouldn't get far. Apparently he knew it, because his shoulders, already slumped from fatigue, drooped further and his gaze lowered to the ground, defeated.

Julian grabbed him by the arm and pulled him toward the building. "Let's go."

Raedrick led the way, swinging the doors open to allow Julian and the brigand to follow easily. Inside was a simple office. Two desks, one on either side of the room facing each other, and a pair of benches on either side of the entrance were the only furnishings. Mounted on the wall behind one of the desks was a rack holding a small collection of swords. A similar rack holding several unstrung bows and an equal number of full quivers hung behind the other. A pair of lamps on wall mounts burned merrily, adding light to the room. A door made of iron bars was set in the wall directly across from the entrance. Julian could see a number of other, similar barred doors in the corridor beyond. Holding cells, no doubt.

A slender man of medium height, with a narrow face and unruly hair the color of hay, sat behind the desk on the left, reviewing a leather-bound ledger. He looked up at once, his eyes widening in surprise, as they walked in. He collected himself quickly, closing the ledger and standing up to greet them.

"Gentlemen. What can I do for you?"

"You the Constable?" Raedrick asked.

The man shook his head. "I'm Deputy Fendig. Constable Malory is off dealing with an issue right now."

"Good enough. This man," Julian pushed the brigand forward as Raedrick gestured toward him, "and several others tried to rob us on the road earlier today. We've brought him here for justice."

Fendig did a double-take and looked the brigand up and down. "Is that right," he said quietly.

There was a long silence as Julian and Raedrick looked at each other. Something very odd was going on, Julian thought.

"That's right," Raedrick said slowly as he looked back at Fendig. "About an hour after noon on the road just above Silver Falls. He and five other…"

"Five?"

"Yeah, five," Julian replied.

Fendig looked doubtful, but he nodded. "Alright." Moving back over to his desk, he pulled open one of the drawers and removed a large iron ring hung with a number of keys. As he stepped past them and unlocked the door to the cell block, he said, "Bring him along."

They followed Fendig into the cell block. Once inside, Julian saw it contained eight cells, four on each side of the corridor. They were all unoccupied. Each cell had a pair of cots and a bucket, no doubt to use as a chamber pot. Narrow windows, too small for a man to squeeze through, let in light. It would be paltry even at noon, but now with dusk coming on the light was virtually non-existent. Only a pair of lamps mounted at either end of the corridor provided illumination. Fendig led them to the last cell on the right and opened the door. It squeaked on its hinges, making Julian wonder how long ago it had been used last.

"In here," Fendig said, gesturing toward the cell.

Raedrick, who was bringing up the rear, stepped forward and pulled out his knife. A quick cut removed the rope that bound the brigand's hands. Then Julian shoved him forward. He stumbled into the cell and fell over onto a cot. For a moment, he just lay there. Then he turned over and sat up. Rubbing his wrists to help restore circulation, the man looked up at Fendig.

"If I were you, I'd think hard about letting me go, Deputy," he said. "I'm with Farzal."

Fendig went pale, and he swallowed audibly. But his voice was steady when he spoke. "That'll be up to the Constable," he said, and he shut the door and locked it. The brigand chuckled softly, a laugh of sadistic amusement. As Fendig walked back to the front office, Julian lingered for a moment to study the prisoner. He did not look half as defeated as he had outside, when he was in Julian and Raedrick's custody.

Back in the front office, Fendig pulled out another ledger and dipped his quill into an inkwell on his desk.

"I'll need your names and where you're staying in town. The…"

"Who or what is Farzal?" Julian asked.

Fendig paused, his quill poised over the paper. Then he sighed and looked up at the two of them. "A band of outlaws has been making trouble in these parts for the last month or so. From their look, they're mostly deserters from the army. Small wonder they turned to thieving, right? Men like that will do anything. Farzal's their leader."

"You're afraid of them," Raedrick said, his tone flat with disapproval.

"Of course not. He's all bluster, that's all." Even if his body language and expression hadn't screamed that he was lying, the speed of Fendig's reply made it plain as day. "Now then, as I said I'll need your names and where you're staying in town. Constable Malory will want to talk to you about this incident."

"Does Molli Millens still run The Oarlock down by the docks?" asked Raedrick.

Fendig looked surprised again, but he nodded. "Yes. Has been for years."

"We'll be staying there."

Raedrick and Julian gave their names, and Fendig thanked them and showed them out with promises that the Constable would contact them first thing in the morning to take their statements.

As the office doors swung shut behind them, Julian shook his head. "Three to one that guy releases our boy before dawn. I'm amazed he even locked him up. Probably wouldn't have if we weren't there."

"I don't know," replied Raedrick. He looked as troubled as Julian felt. "Nothing we can do about it though. Let's go get settled and warm up."

It was hard to argue with that idea.

Chapter Five

The Oarlock

The Oarlock turned out to be a fair-sized Inn a block and a half away from the docks. Two stories tall, it was a simple building, and far from new, but it had obviously been well-maintained over the years by a very conscientious owner. A simple sign, showing a bearded man in foul weather gear pulling on the oars of a rowboat in rough seas with the Inn's name written in the waves, hung from a wrought-iron stanchion on the street.

Raedrick needed no directions to find it. He led Julian to the Inn's stables as quickly as if he had been going between the Constable's office and the Inn every day for his whole life. Julian thought he knew what made Raedrick tick after all the time they had spent together at the front, but his familiarity with the Vale and its inhabitants had come as a surprise. He reminded himself to ask about it after they were settled and nursing a tankard.

The interior was not very much different from any other

Inn Julian had visited. A long wooden bar rested along the wall to his right as he walked inside. Tables with chairs for four lay scattered around the room, and there were a half dozen booths built into the wall to his left. A set of swinging doors in the back no doubt led into the kitchen and a stairwell in the left rear corner led upstairs. Two fireplaces, one in each of the front corners, provided warmth and some light. About two dozen customers sat around the various tables or on stools at the bar. One table in particular, in the right rear corner of the taproom, was particularly popular. Seven men and a lone woman clustered around it. A dice game, unless Julian missed his guess. Two powerfully built men sat on stools at either end of the bar. The fact that they were facing away from the taps and toward the rest of the room screamed that they were bouncers.

Raedrick made a beeline for the bar. Julian followed more slowly. The bartender was a balding man in his early middle years. He had the bland look of a man who had listened to enough drunkards to no longer pay any mind to what they have to say. Raedrick waved him over, but he took his time in coming over. When he finally arrived, the bartender looked Raedrick, then Julian, up and down and sniffed.

"Looking for a room, eh boys?"

Raedrick looked around the room again before answering. "Is Molli here tonight?"

The bartender nodded. "She is. She's dealing with something right now, though, but I can set you up."

Raedrick shook his head. "We'll wait for her, thanks."

The bartender shrugged and turned away. That wouldn't do at all. Julian spoke up. "We'll take a drink while we wait."

"Yeah? What'll it be?" The bartender sounded annoyed. His expression as he looked back at them over his shoulder confirmed it.

Julian said, "Mulled wine." He glanced at Raedrick and added, "Two of them."

The bartender nodded and moved away to the center of the bar, where several tapped casks sat on their sides. He returned a short time later with two steaming tankards and sat them down on the bar in front of Raedrick. "Two pennies," he said.

Raedrick fished a couple coins from his pouch and paid the man, then handed one of the tankards to Julian. The aroma of the mulling spices combined with the wine's natural nose made Julian's mouth water, and he suddenly realized how hungry he was. Not surprising considering their small, hurried lunch earlier. "Probably ought to get some dinner, too," he said before taking a drink. The wine was just as good as he anticipated, bringing a smile to his lips.

"Yes, definitely. But first I'd like to..."

Raedrick broke off as a portly woman with grey hair tied in a bun atop her head stepped into the room from the kitchens. She wore a simple dress with a bright white apron over top and took a moment to survey the taproom before heading over to the bar. She conferred with the bartender for a moment. He gestured down the bar toward Julian and Raedrick and she looked over at them, her expression one of curiosity. Then she said something else, which the bartender acknowledged with a nod, and made her way toward them. She stopped along the way to exchange pleasantries with a group of customers and was still chuckling from something they said when she reached Julian and Raedrick. Wiping her hands on her apron, she looked them up and down for a moment before speaking.

"I'm Molli. What can I do for you?"

"We're looking for a room..." Julian began, but Raedrick cut him off.

"You may not remember, but you used to do business with my father. Roland Baletier?"

"Baletier." Molli repeated the name slowly, as though she was tasting every syllable. Then her eyes widened. "Woodworker who traveled with Crispin Thunderly." She smiled, a broad grin that changed her expression from severe and businesslike to warm and inviting. "Why, you wouldn't be little Raedrick would you?" At his nod, she laughed and clapped him on his arms then pulled him in for a hug. "Well look at you, boy. All grown up! What brings you back through these parts?"

"Heading home from the front."

Molli's mirth faded. "Well. I'm glad you're able to. I've heard it's brutal out on the front lines."

She had no idea, Julian though. If she knew half of what had happened out there... Well, she didn't, and he had no intention of describing it. Neither did Raedrick, apparently, as he simply shrugged and looked away. Julian knew him well enough to recognize the guarded expression that hinted at emotion ready to burst out in a torrent.

Clearing his throat, Julian said, "Mistress Millens, I'm Julian Hinderbrook," and offered her his hand.

Molli turned to him and shook his hand with a warm smile. "My pleasure, Julian. Call me Molli. You and Raedrick know each other from the Army, I assume?"

"Yes, ma'am. We finished with the Army at the same time, and he told me so many good things about Mol Teribor that I decided to come along to see what the fuss was about."

"Is that where your father keeps himself these days?" she asked, looking back at Raedrick. "I haven't heard from him in...ten years? Fifteen? I hope he's well."

Raedrick had his emotions under control again. He smiled and made a dismissive gesture. "He always finds a way to do

32

well. I haven't heard from him in six months or so, but last I heard he was on the verge of making a killing in some business deal or other."

Shaking her head, Molli laughed merrily. "That sounds like him." Stepping back, she looked them over again. "Well. Looks like you two could use a bath, a meal, and a bed. You're in luck: I have one more room empty. Follow me."

Molli led them up the staircase at the back of the taproom. It was a tough climb, with every step painfully straining the stitches in Julian's thigh. He took his time, but even still he wasn't at all certain he hadn't pulled some of the stitches out by the time he reached the top. Molli eyed him askance as he stepped, breathing hard from the pain, off the landing.

"A strapping young man like you shouldn't have so much trouble with one flight of stairs," she quipped. "What's wrong with your leg?"

"Brigands on the road," he replied through gritted teeth. "Got me in the thigh."

Molli's eyes narrowed as she looked down at Julian's leg. "Where did this happen?"

"Just above the falls," Raedrick replied. "We brought one of them in to the Constable before we came here."

Molli mumbled something under her breath. Julian was not really surprised to hear a few salty curses in there, ladylike or not. She did run a tavern, after all. More loudly, she said, "Farzal's bunch?" They nodded. "Figures. Well, you're safe now. Come on."

She set off down the hall, leaving Julian and Raedrick to look quizzically at each other.

"That was awfully fatalistic," Julian said.

Raedrick nodded. "The Molli I remember was no-nonsense. Wouldn't tolerate trouble from anyone." His eyes moved to follow Molli as she moved down the hall. "First the deputy and now Molli. Who is this Farzal fellow?"

"Dunno. But it's not our problem, is it?" Julian limped down the hall after Molli. He glanced over his shoulder several paces on. Raedrick hadn't moved from an inch, and he wore a very troubled expression.

* * * * *

Their room was all the way at the end of the hall on the left, just before the hall made a turn to the right. It was about the same as every other room Julian had ever rented out. It had two narrow beds against the wall on opposite sides of the room, a locking chest at the foot of each bed, a chest of drawers beneath the window, a hanging wardrobe in one corner, and a washbasin and mirror in the other. The window was curtained and constructed so the lower half could be opened outward. All in all, not too bad.

Molli smiled apologetically as she showed them the room. "I wish my premium rooms were available for you boys," she said, "but they were rented out two days ago. I hope this will be ok?"

"It's perfect, ma'am," Julian said. Raedrick echoed him, and Molli smiled a bit more broadly.

"The baths are across the hall, and the privy is around the corner," she said. "When you've cleaned up, come downstairs and I'll have dinner ready for you."

"Thank you, Molli," Raedrick said.

"It's great to see you again," she replied. She turned to leave, but before closing the door behind her, she looked over her shoulder and gave Raedrick a conspiratorial look. "Don't be too long. Lani should be back soon, and I know she'll want to catch up."

Molli pulled the door shut. The click of the latch sounded

solid and, for some reason, comforting.

Julian tossed his saddlebag onto his bed and began removing his belongings from the pouches. "Who's Lani?" he asked.

Raedrick was still looking at the door. At Julian's words, he gave a start then, smiling abashedly, set about unpacking. "She's Molli's daughter. We used to play together when my father and I came through here. She used to say I was her best friend." He paused for a moment. "I always liked her, but..." Raedrick looked over at Julian and shrugged. "She was also a bit odd. I didn't understand how I could be her best friend, since we came through so infrequently."

Julian shrugged. "Girls are hard to understand sometimes."

"That's an understatement."

"I thought you said your father owned a ranch in the hills above Mol Teribor. How did you come to pass through here so often?"

Raedrick paused again. "He does now. For a long time, though, he made his living as a woodworker. He made high quality tools, furniture, and toys that his friend Crispin sold from city to city. After my mother died, he couldn't bear to stay in our town anymore. So he convinced Crispin that they could make more money if he joined the caravan and made his products continually on the road. And he was right. The money flowed like never before. But more than money, we made many great friends, like Molli and Lani. Of course, we eventually got tired of traveling all the time. In truth, I think he tired of it before I did." Chuckling softly, Raedrick looked back at Julian and grinned. "But that might be because he met a lovely young widow whose late husband was a big-time rancher."

Julian chuckled as well. "I can understand that. Glad to

hear it all worked out."

Raedrick nodded. "It did."

Chapter Six

Night Life

After a bath, Julian felt much better. The previous few weeks had been draining, and had filled him with tension he almost hadn't realized. To say nothing of grime from the road and his physical injuries. He could have soaked all night and to blazes with going back down to the taproom, but eventually the bath water cooling and his stomach growling forced him to get up.

Raedrick had already finished dressing and gone back downstairs when Julian returned to their room from the baths, so he lingered just long enough to change out his bandages and don a fresh set of clothes before heading downstairs himself.

It was a lot easier on his leg going down than coming up. No big surprise there.

He found Raedrick sitting at a table not far from the bar with Molli and a pretty blond-haired girl. They spied him as he approached and waved him over with a trio of smiles. As he took a seat at the table, Raedrick spoke in an excited voice.

"Julian, this is Lani Millens, Molli's daughter."

Lani was even prettier up close than she had been from afar. She was not terribly tall, best as he could tell with her sitting down, but her warm smile, rosy cheeks, full bosom, and intelligent gaze was enchanting. Julian smiled broadly as he shook hands with her and brought his lips down to the back of her hand.

"The pleasure is all mine," he said.

Lani giggled, glancing aside at Raedrick. "You weren't kidding," she said in a melodic alto.

Julian looked askance at his friend. "What did you say to her?"

"Only that you're a rascal who likes to flirt," Molli said.

"Great. Well, that's not true." He smiled a bit more broadly. "I'm not at all a rascal."

Both ladies laughed merrily for a moment, then Molli stood up.

"I'll go check on dinner. It should be ready by now. Please make yourself comfortable, Julian. Tonight's on me."

That was music to his ears.

* * * * *

Dinner was outstanding. Braised beef atop seasoned rice, with steaming bread fresh from the oven and a very nice bottle of wine from the Pyreen Valley, followed by a large slice of a kind of cake Julian had never had before. It was unbelievably delicious, though, and was a fitting end to the meal.

Conversation was muted at first, since Julian and Raedrick were both famished and did little more than shovel food down their throats. But eventually, after the plates were all pushed aside, the talk picked up a bit.

Unfortunately for Julian, however, the conversation quickly degenerated into Raedrick and Lani exchanging cherished anecdotes from their childhood dalliance. Or whatever it was. Julian quickly began to feel that his presence was no longer needed, especially after Molli left to tend to business, so he begged off to run to the privy. Neither Raedrick nor Lani objected.

In truth, he was feeling the call of nature. But when he returned to the taproom after satisfying that particular need, he looked over at the table and saw the two of them engrossed in conversation and lost in each others' eyes, and he turned away toward the bar. Far be it for him to block his friend's chance to do well with a pretty lady.

Julian slid onto a stool next to an older man in a faded wool cloak and tried to flag down the bartender. The man was busy at the far end of the bar, though, so Julian was forced to wait.

"You're one of them two newcomers, the ones who brought the thief in this evening, right?" The man sitting next to him had turned to look at him, and addressed him in a tone of friendly curiosity.

"Sure am. Julian." He held out his hand and received a good firm handshake in response.

"Horace. Damn good to meet you, boy. 'Bout time someone did something about them scumbags."

"It's wasn't much, really. Just defending ourselves is all."

Horace snorted. "Way I hear tell, you two boys fought off a dozen of them bandits without taking a scratch. Don't sound like nothing to me."

Julian looked incredulously at him for a moment, then burst out laughing. "First of all, there were six. Secondly," he gestured toward his thigh, then held up his bandaged right hand and pointed to his nose, "I took more than a couple scratches. Now, my friend over there," he nodded in Raedrick's direction, "he got off without a hitch. But I had the tougher task in that fight."

Horace snorted again. "Well, whatever. Point is, you boys did real good, and I'm proud to know you."

"Thanks, Horace. I appreciate that."

The bartender finally made it over to Julian, and he ordered another tankard of mulled wine. But when the bartender brought the drink, Horace spoke up again.

"I'm paying for that, Rolf. In fact, this boy and his friend don't pay for another drink tonight, understand? It's on me."

Rolf looked quizzically at Horace, then shrugged. "However you want to play it, Horace. I'll put it on your tab."

"That's really not necessary…" Julian began, but Horace waved him to silence.

"The hell it ain't. You boys did us a public service today. Least I can do is buy you a couple drinks."

Julian realized arguing any further would be futile. Besides, who was he to pass up free drinks, especially if they were for doing something that really wasn't anything special at all. Smiling, he raised his tankard to Horace and said, "In that case, thank you, kind sir. I…"

A movement at the other end of the room drew Julian's eye, and he lost track of what he was about to say. The woman descending the stairs from the second floor was hard to miss. Long wavy black hair, a perfectly hourglass-shaped figure, and a pretty face, she would have stood out anywhere. But here, the fine fabric of her dress and the glitter of precious metal and gems reflecting the firelight from her wrists, ears, and neck stood out and marked her as a lady of means. Julian couldn't help but stare.

Horace noticed, of course, and followed Julian's gaze with his own. Then he burst out laughing.

"Forget about it, boy. That girl ain't got no interest in the likes of you and me."

"Is that so. What makes you say that?"

Horace looked at him as though he was daft. "Well look at her!"

Rolling his eyes, Julian returned Horace's gaze with one of incredulity. "That's it?" he asked, and realized that he had just let a healthy dose of annoyance slip through into the tone he was using to address the man who was buying his drinks. He cleared his throat and looked away. But if Horace was put out or offended, it didn't show in his demeanor or in how he treated the question.

"A well set-up lass like her probably comes from nobility, has a rich husband, or is looking for one. *That's* it."

The woman walked, or rather flowed, over to an empty table near one of the fireplaces and sat down. Julian noted with interest that she sat with her back to the wall. She was a careful one, or so it seemed. She had barely settled into her chair when a server hurried over. They exchanged quick words then, making a slight curtsy, the server made her way quickly back to the bar.

"Let's see if your theory is true," Julian said to Horace. Then he stood and moved over to where the server stood waiting for the woman's drink.

Horace chuckled. "Your funeral, boy."

Julian reached the server as she was reaching for the drink. Moving quickly, he got his hand in ahead of her and snatched it up then tossed a few coins onto the bar.

"Hey!"

"I've got this one, thanks," Julian said over his shoulder as he moved away from the bar. The mixture of chagrin and bemusement on the server's face was classic.

He reached the woman's table quickly, only having to pause once to avoid being run over by a large drunk fellow on his way to the privy. She was reading from a small leather-bound book as he approached. From a distance, she looked attractive. Close up, she was gorgeous. Stunning, even. Suddenly struck by a big case of nerves, Julian almost turned around and went back to Horace at the bar.

None of that.

Taking a deep breath, Julian squared his shoulders and strode the last few paces to the woman's table.

"Your drink, my lady," he said as he placed her glass onto the table in front of her.

The woman didn't look up. She just murmured, "Thank you," and held out a coin. A silver coin. Again, Julian was tempted to just walk away, after pocketing the money, of course. Instead, he sat down in an empty chair at her table.

"No need for that. I covered this one."

She looked up from her book and frowned. Julian moved ahead before she could say anything.

"I'm Julian Hinderbrook. And your name is…?" He put on his most charming smile as he spoke, the one that normally made the maidens swoon.

"None of your business." She inserted a place mark, snapped her book shut, and cast it down on the table with an expression of disgust. "It's bad enough I'm stranded in this flyspeck of a town in the middle of nowhere. I don't need to be accosted by every bumpkin in the place. Thank you for the drink. Now, off with you." She made a shooing gesture that carried entire levels of contemptuous dismissal.

Julian had to force his smile not to compress into a scowl. Why that conceited little… "I'm no bumpkin." He knew his tone was frosty, but he couldn't help it and, frankly, she deserved it.

The woman rolled her eyes. "Yes, of course. How could I have missed it? You're a cultural minister from Tyrash." Sarcasm dripped from her words. It didn't help that Julian had no idea where Tyrash was. All of a sudden he felt stupid, and from her expression he looked the part, too. She shook her head slightly then picked up her book again and opened it up to her place. Making another shooing gesture, she began to read again.

A lesser man would have departed at this point. Julian decided to make one last attempt.

"Look, I'm just trying to be friendly here. I…"

As he began speaking, the woman looked up at him through narrowed eyes that sparkled with irritation. She cupped her hand in front of her mouth as though she was going to blow him a kiss. But when she blew out, instead of a kiss a plume of flame leapt out toward him.

Julian shouted a curse and pushed himself backwards, his hands flying upwards to protect his face. He leaned way back and his chair teetered for a moment, then fell over onto the ground, taking him with it. The flame burned out very quickly; it did not even reach his position where he had been sitting. But the flash of heat was real. Very real. Julian lay there on the floor for a moment, stunned.

A sudden silence descended on the taproom as Julian pushed himself up to his feet. Every eye was fixed on him and the woman. His face warm with embarrassment and from the brief heat from the flame, he fixed the woman with a glare as he brushed himself off. Then he turned and walked away. From the corner of his eye, he saw her give a mocking little wave as he left. He did not look back.

Horace looked as stunned as Julian felt when he returned

to the bar. All the same, he managed a smirk as he said, "Told you so."

"You could have warned me she was a mage," Julian replied angrily before he downed a large drink of his wine.

Horace sniffed. "She ain't no mage. Women ain't allowed to study magery, boy. Wonder how and where she picked that up."

Julian shrugged and drank again, finishing off his tankard. Slamming it down onto the bar, he scowled over at the woman for a moment. "Whatever. I've had enough for one day. Good meeting you, Horace."

Horace chuckled and shook Julian's hand again. "Don't let it get to you. Good night."

Julian nodded slowly and made his way to the stairs. As he began to ascend, he looked back over his shoulder for a moment. The woman was still there, looking just as pretty as before, and just as separate. For a heartbeat, he imagined their eyes met and she smiled briefly.

Chapter Seven

Opportunity Knocks

Julian and Raedrick awoke with the dawn the next morning. When they came downstairs, Julian was surprised to find the taproom all but deserted. A young man stood behind the bar and a single serving girl lounged on a barstool near him. Besides them, one man sat alone in one of the booths and another two sat together at the same table the mage lady used the night before.

It took a few minutes after they sat down for the server to notice Julian and Raedrick's presence. She sauntered over hurriedly, her hips making a nice swaying motion as she moved, and spoke in an apologetic tone.

"Good morning. I'm Celine. I'm sorry to keep you gentlemen waiting. We don't get very many customers this early."

"No worries, Celine," Raedrick said with a smile. "We're just looking for some tea and breakfast."

Celine returned Raedrick's smile and nodded, then swayed away to the kitchens. It was hard for Julian to move his gaze away from her hips, but she soon passed out of sight as the kitchen door swung shut behind her. Ah well. He looked back at his friend instead.

"So Raedrick, what's the deal with Lani?"

"What do you mean?"

"She was pretty into you last night."

Raedrick snorted and waved off Julian's remark. "We were good friends for a long time and had a lot of catching up to do. Of course she was excited about it; so was I."

"Whatever you say."

Celine returned then, carrying a tray that held a teapot, two cups, and a jar with two spoons. Smiling professionally at them, she set a cup in front of each of them and placed the teapot and jar in the center of the table. Then she said, "Your breakfast will be out in a moment," and left them to return to the bar.

Curious, Julian opened the jar while Raedrick poured the tea. It was full of honey. Perfect. He took two dollops and set the jar back down where Raedrick could use it, then stirred his cup.

Getting back to the subject at hand, Julian asked, "So you're saying you'd tell her no if she offered to... you know." He left the rest of the thought go unspoken, instead grinning at his friend as he quirked one eyebrow upwards.

Raedrick flushed but didn't say anything. The silence spoke volumes.

"I didn't think so."

The room brightened noticeably as the front door swung open, admitting the morning's sunlight far more effectively than the few windows in the walls did. Julian turned in his chair, his eyes drawn to the glow of the doorway as two men stepped inside. Both were tall men; they easily had a hand on Raedrick, and he wasn't short. But he wasn't able to make out much more about them until the door swung shut and the glare from outside subsided.

The man on the right was plump, with carefully trimmed hair that had gone grey at the temples. His clothing was plain, but the fabric was obviously of high quality, and he wore a golden pin of some sort over his left breast. The other man was more lean. He was bald and wore the clothing of a working man, except for the silver pin he wore over his breast and the baldric that hung across his body from shoulder to hip, which housed a short weapon of some sort. Probably a sword breaker, from its shape.

The two men paused inside the front door and surveyed the room. Then the lean one nudged the other and nodded in Julian and Raedrick's direction. They moved toward the table in a deliberate, businesslike pace.

"Who are these fellows?" Julian wondered aloud, earning a shrug of ignorance from his friend in reply.

He didn't have long to wait to find out. The two men arrived at the table quickly. Up close, he could see that the plump man's pin was in the shape of a fish jumping out of the water. The silver pin the other wore was shaped like a pair of scales dangling from a clenched fist.

"Raedrick Baletier and Julian Hinderbrook?" It was the leaner of the two who spoke first.

The two friends nodded in unison.

"I am Lucian Malory, the Constable. This is Wilford Brimly, the mayor of this town." Constable Malory gestured to the two empty chairs at the table. "May we join you?"

Julian and Raedrick exchanged glances. The Constable wasn't a big surprise, but what did the mayor want with them? From all the hints the previous evening, Julian knew

Raedrick was curious and troubled about what was going on in town. And, truth be told, Julian was as well. It wasn't often he got called a hero for stringing up a single robber. What could it hurt to hear what these two had to say?

Julian shrugged, and Raedrick replied, "Please do."

The two men settled into the chairs and collected themselves quickly. Mayor Brimly wasted no time in getting to the point.

"You gents did a great thing for this town last night when you brought that thug in for justice."

"Oh?" Raedrick affected a surprised tone, though Julian was sure he was no more surprised than he was himself. Enough people had made a fuss over that fellow already, after all.

Mayor Brimly nodded emphatically. "Absolutely. You two are the first who've been able to strike back at Farzal's gang in any meaningful way. I can't tell you how much higher people's spirits are this morning, since the word of your deed spread around."

Constable Malory looked sidelong at the Mayor as he spoke, his expression a bit less enthusiastic. When the Mayor finished talking, he cleared his throat and cut in, looking back at Julian and Raedrick. "Fendig passed your story on to me, but there are a number of details that need to be filled in, if you don't mind answering a few questions."

"Why would we mind?" Julian could think of several reasons without straining, but they had decided on how to answer certain questions a long time ago, so there probably wouldn't be much harm in it. All the same, he wished Raedrick didn't sound so eager.

Constable Malory inclined his head, in a gesture Julian was sure was meant to portray gratitude, but it ended up appearing condescendingly superior. Irritation rose within

Julian, but he forced it down. This wasn't a time to go off half-cocked.

"You say the attack occurred just above the falls, on the river road. How many attackers were there?"

"Six."

The Constable looked down his nose at them, doubt plain on his face. "That's what you told Fendig. He didn't believe it, and neither do I. Four, maybe, but six? Farzal's men are too good for that."

Julian snorted, not waiting for Raedrick to reply. "Good? They were careless. Sloppy. Only one of them was worth a damn."

"The man you brought in?"

Julian shook his head. "No. He was the first to fall, and he's damn lucky all I did was kick him."

The Constable and Mayor exchanged long looks. The Mayor's eyes gleamed with an eager light, but Malory held up a calming hand, silencing him before he could speak.

"What brings you boys into town," the Constable asked as he looked back to Julian and Raedrick. "Not many folks come through this way anymore. Hell, almost no one does unless they're part of a merchant's caravan, and most of them take the southern routes now too."

"It was time to come home from the Army, and I didn't want to take the extra time to circle around to the south. Julian's heard me talk about Mol Teribor enough that he decided to come along since he was leaving at the same time." Raedrick told the tale quickly, but in an earnest enough tone that Julian found himself halfway believing it, even though he knew better.

The Constable's eyes narrowed. "You boys been out on the front?"

They both nodded.

"I heard they were canceling people's release from enlistment until the end of hostilities. How is it you got out?"

"We heard that too, a few days after we left," Julian replied. "We've been thanking our lucky stars that we didn't leave a week later than we did."

Constable Malory pursed his lips in thought for a moment, then he nodded and leaned back in his chair. He turned to look at Mayor Brimly and gave a little nod.

Beaming, Mayor Brimly moved his chair closer to the table. "I'd like to hire you boys."

"I beg your pardon," Julian replied.

"The town needs good men on our side if we're going to get rid of Farzal's gang. You two seem like ideal candidates for the job. What do you say?"

Chapter Eight

Employment

J ulian was speechless. How was he supposed to react to that?

Raedrick, as usual, was quick on his feet. "Why don't you start with telling us who this Farzal person is."

Mayor Brimly looked disappointed as he sat back in his chair, but the Constable's eyes were understanding. In point of fact, Julian could swear the doubt he had seen in the man's eyes faded when Raedrick asked the question. What, did he think they were a couple of rank amateurs, who would take a job without knowing what it entailed? Apparently, he had. Or at least he had feared they were. Julian wasn't sure which was worse.

"A month and a half ago," Malory said, "a merchant caravan pulled into town with one carriage burned and two men dead. They told of being attacked by robbers in

Holbart's Pass. A few days later, a delivery man working for one of the craftsmen in town discovered one of the outlying farmsteads had been burned down. Since then, the attacks have come more frequently, and against larger targets. Last week, they hit a farm not far from here, down by the Eastflow. A calling card at the scene claimed Glimmer Vale in Farzal's name and said that unless we paid a regular tribute, things would get worse. Then four days ago, a merchant caravan was completely destroyed on its way through Holbart's pass. There were only two survivors: a lady who managed to escape the battle and a caravan guard who we found barely clinging to life."

Malory's eyebrow quirked upward. "And yesterday you were attacked. This is the first time we've seen activity from them on that side of the Vale, and it proves they are becoming more comfortable with their position. It's also the first time anyone has managed to defeat them to date."

Mayor Brimly spoke again. "Lydelton lives and dies by the traffic coming through the passes. Our population has dwindled in recent years as merchant traffic has shifted south. If these bandits are allowed to continue unchecked, before long no one will make the transit at all and we will lose everything we have. We must put a stop to these attacks. And we need your help to do so."

"Why don't you just pay the tribute?" Julian asked.

Mayor Brimly looked shocked. "Give in to these thugs?"

"It's better than being burned out."

He shook his head vigorously. "No! Even if we had the funds they demanded, it's a question of honor!"

"But the fact is we don't have the money," Constable Malory interjected. "Even a large city would be hard pressed to come up with the sum they demanded on a monthly basis, and we are far from being a large city."

"Have you tried negotiating with them?"

Malory snorted. "With whom? The man you brought in is the first of Farzal's band anyone has seen and lived to tell of it."

"Then you don't really know what you're dealing with," Raedrick said. "For all you know, it could have only been those six fellows lurking in the pass this whole time. Six men with bows can do a lot of damage in the right place."

The Constable again shook his head. "No, the survivors of the last merchant caravan described an attacking force of at least thirty to forty men."

"So you see why we must have your help?" Mayor Brimly's voice trembled slightly.

"No," Julian replied, "I don't see that. You don't really know what you're up against yet. If you want my advice, I'd say you should give that man we brought in a counter-offer, one you can afford to pay, and have him deliver it to Farzal. Unless he's a total fool, he'll take it, and you can avoid a major confrontation." He looked from the Constable to the Mayor and back. "Or do you think you can win a pitched battle against them?"

The Constable shook his head. "It's just me and Fendig here in town. In the summer months, I sometimes hire some of the tougher lads from the nearby farms or off the fishing boats to help keep order while the caravans are in town. That's all we've ever needed until now."

"Then you're in no position to not pay. I..."

"We'll do it," Raedrick said, to Julian's chagrin but not to his complete surprise.

"I'm not sure..." he began, but Raedrick cut him off.

"We'll do it." Raedrick gave him a firm, no-nonsense look as he repeated the words.

Julian met Raedrick's stare for a moment. He knew that

expression. Raedrick always wore it on the way into battle.

"Will you give us a minute, gentlemen?" Julian asked, not looking at the Constable and the Mayor. Out of the corner of his eye, he saw them nod and leave the table. He gave them a minute to walk out of earshot, then he spoke again.

"What the hell are you doing?"

"These people need our help, Julian."

Julian rolled his eyes. "No, they need help from a company of soldiers, not..." He looked around quickly. No one was close enough to hear. All the same, he leaned closer and spoke in a whisper. "Not from two guys on the run. We need to be putting as many miles behind us as we can. We can't afford to get caught up in this sort of thing."

Raedrick's eyes flashed with anger. Julian raised a placating hand and continued quickly.

"Look, I get it. You've got nice memories of this place from when you were a kid. But it's not our problem. And even if it was, the two of us can't make a difference here. Not against forty men."

"We can and you know it. We just took out six of them without much trouble."

Julian snorted. "I'm out of action for a week or two thanks to that little meeting, in case you forgot," he said, pointing at his thigh. "Yet another reason we can't and shouldn't do this."

"Rubbish," Raedrick replied. "You heal quickly. And it's not like we're going to charge off to fight them all at once, right this minute. It'll take time to get intel and prepare before we can expect any action."

Julian opened his mouth to reply, but Raedrick spoke over him.

"I'm going to help. You can leave if you want, I suppose. But do you really think you'll make it out of the Vale?"

"What are you talking about?"

"They're ambushing people traveling through the passes, remember? I doubt they'll just let you go."

Raedrick's words hit like a ton of bricks. Julian had to admit that hit upon a point he had not considered. He took it as a given that the two of them could just move along. But if Raedrick was right, they were stuck here. Son of a bitch.

"Hadn't thought of that, had you?" Raedrick asked. He didn't have to sound so satisfied about it.

Julian shook his head.

"The way I see it, if we can't leave, we're now part of this community. So yes, this is our problem. And I'm going to help solve it. This is the sort of thing I thought I'd be doing in the Army, but never did. Didn't you?"

Julian looked away from his friend. As his gaze panned around the taproom, he noted the tension, and the hope, in the Mayor's face. The suppressed fear in the bartender's. The determination, tinged with hopelessness, in the Constable's. Yes, this was exactly the sort of thing the Army claimed to do, and was supposed to do. Defending those who could not defend themselves.

Damn it all.

"Ok, I'm in. Hope we don't live to regret this."

Raedrick chuckled. "Don't worry. If it goes wrong, we won't live to do anything at all."

That was not very comforting.

Chapter Nine

Working Arrangements

Mayor Brimly bubbled over with enthusiasm when Julian and Raedrick announced their acceptance of the offer. He shook both their hands repeatedly, fairly bouncing up and down each time he did.

"Thank you, gentlemen. Thank you! The people of Lydelton will honor your names always."

He sure was laying it on a bit thick, considering they hadn't really done anything yet. Julian found it understandable to an extent; the town had been living in fear for weeks. But still, he couldn't help but wonder how true the Mayor's gratitude really was.

Constable Malory was more reserved, merely nodding with a small smile. Again, appropriate. It was the Mayor's place to be boisterous, and from what Julian had seen they all tended to enjoy it. The Constable had a serious job, though, and that tended to attract more serious, business-minded men to it.

Finally, Mayor Brimly took a step back. "You'll report to Lucian on this, but I'll be keeping tabs on how things are going. For now, I'll leave you to get better acquainted." He beamed a smile at them and added, "Good luck to us all!" Then he turned and strolled out of the Inn.

"Well he's plenty enthusiastic," Raedrick quipped.

"Mayor Brimly cares very deeply for the people of this town," Constable Malory said.

Just then, the waitress came out of the kitchen, carrying a tray with two plates, a pitcher, and two cups on it. She approached the table, but paused when she saw the Constable standing next to them. She looked between Julian, Raedrick, and Malory with a questioning expression on her face.

The Constable noted her presence and gestured for her to get about her work, saying, "I'll not interrupt your breakfast any longer. Come by my office after you've dined and we'll discuss the situation in more detail."

Breakfast consisted of chopped up fried potatoes, a hunk of bread smeared with butter, and fish meat baked in a sweet batter, along with spiced cider. Julian had noticed in their short time in town that the locals seemed to put fish into just about everything. That was understandable, he supposed, considering the proximity of the lake and its obvious contribution to the local economy. Still, fish for breakfast struck him as odd.

It was tasty though. He couldn't complain about that.

"I hope you know what you're doing," Julian said as he and Raedrick tromped upstairs to retrieve their equipment. His thigh began to sting again, causing him to question his decision.

Raedrick responded with a soft snort and a shrug of his shoulders. "You know as much as I do."

Julian rolled his eyes. Yeah, this was going to end up being a bad idea.

A few minutes later, after they donned their mail and strapped on their weapons, the two friends headed out. In midmorning, Lydelton was markedly different than it had been the previous evening. More people were out and about, conducting the errands of the day. To the right as they exited the inn, the road became more congested quickly as it descended to the lakeshore and the docks. A dozen or more boats were tied up along the lone pier in sight. A line of men stood around next to each boat on the dock, helping offload large bundled items in a daisy train leading to a warehouse at the head of the pier.

The scene struck Julian as a bit odd. "A little early to be offloading isn't it?"

Raedrick followed Julian's gaze toward the dock. A confused expression on his face, he shrugged his shoulders before replying. "I would think so. I wonder what's going on?"

There was no particular hurry to get to the Constable's office, so the two men set off toward the docks. The road descended quickly, and before long they reached the warehouse building. The line of workers entered through a side door, but Julian and Raedrick opted for the main entrance.

Within, the warehouse was larger than it appeared from the outside. The ground level consisted mostly of a single large room with a vaulted ceiling. A number of large bins stood at intervals around the room. The workers came in through the side and walked to specific bins. There they unwrapped their packages and dumped the contents, fish of course, into the bins. As Raedrick and Julian watched, one of the bins became filled to capacity, and a man standing near it pulled on a rope. A bell rang overhead and, a moment later, another pair of workers entered the room, pushing a bin before them. It was only then that Julian noticed that each bin was wheeled. The two new men replaced the full bin with their empty one and pushed it toward the rear of the warehouse, where a wide pair of swinging doors separated this room from another.

"Hey, what are you doing in here?"

The voice, gruff and businesslike, drew Julian's eye to a tall stocky man who was approaching from the left. The man was in his early middle years and wore his greying black hair cut short. He wore work boots and coveralls like the other men, but his shirt was red while theirs were blue. Julian surmised he was the foreman.

"We were just curious about your setup here," Julian said, putting on a friendly smile. "Seems a bit early to be offloading the boats. The day's not even a third done."

The foreman scowled. "It's almost done for this shift. Fish don't jump except at twilight, so the boats go out before sunrise and at sunset to catch them." He looked them up and down, his eyes lingering on the sword at Julian's hip and Raedrick's saber. "Don't see what that matters to you. You don't have the look of men looking for a job."

"We're not."

"Then get out. This is a business, not a tourist attraction." He pointed with authority toward the door they had entered through.

There wasn't any point to objecting, so they left.

* * * * *

It took about ten minutes to walk to Constable Malory's office from the fish warehouse. By the end of the walk,

Julian's thigh was throbbing again. Each step caused him to grit his teeth. This was no way for a big hero to start off his job as savior.

Constable Malory was seated behind the desk to the right as they walked in the door, perusing a small collection of official-looking papers. He looked up as they entered and nodded in greeting.

"I was just going over the reports of all the raids to date. I thought maybe you would like to review them as well. Might be there's something we missed."

That made sense, Julian supposed. He moved over to the desk to pick up one of the reports, but Raedrick's words brought him up short.

"Where is the prisoner?"

Julian turned to see his friend looking into the cell block. His eyes widened when he noticed what Raedrick was talking about: all the cell doors were open. Julian turned back to the Constable, a simmering anger beginning to well up within him. What had these people done?

Then Constable Malory spoke, dousing Julian's anger as quickly as it flared up. "Fendig has him down at the courthouse for his preliminary hearing with the judge. They should be back in an hour or so."

"I didn't realize you have the resources for a full inquiry and trial here, as remote as you are," Raedrick replied as Julian picked up the stack of reports.

"Due process is still due process, wherever you are," Constable Malory said, his lips turning downwards into a slight frown.

"I didn't mean to imply…" Raedrick began, but Constable Malory cut him off.

"You did more than just imply it. You flat out stated that…"

The argument faded into the background as Julian picked up the reports and began reading.

The first was the deposition from a month and a half ago by a fellow named Modrin Gilanty, of Holis, over by the Great Sea. He owned a trading company and had been traversing Holbart's pass when he was accosted by half a dozen men who were equipped similarly to the brigands Julian and Raedrick encountered the previous day. Gilanty reported that his guards had repelled the attack but one of his carriages had been burned to the ground, along with all of its wares, and two of his men killed. Total loss: 200 marks, including contractual reparations he now owed to the families of his lost men. Julian winced; that much money would keep twenty families eating for a year in many areas of the kingdom.

That was bad. The next report was worse. Julian knew what to expect from what Malory had told them back at the Inn, but the deposition went into more details. Lev Harpwell was the man who discovered the burned out farmstead during a run to deliver horseshoes from the Gil Aberdyn, one of the two blacksmiths in town. What he described... It made the burned out farm Julian and Raedrick came across seem civilized, by comparison. What was wrong with these people?

The reports continued, almost a full dozen of them spanning the time between the first caravan attack and the attack above the falls yesterday.

Julian replaced the last report before his and Raedrick's back down on Constable Malory's desk and suppressed a slight shiver. This was not going to be easy. He looked over at Raedrick, who was reading an earlier report, and shook his head.

"All of a sudden I've got a bad feeling about this."

Raedrick looked up, one eyebrow quirking upward as he responded. "You had a good feeling before?"

"You know what I mean. The lady who gave this last report said there were dozens of attackers. We'll need a bloody army to fight them off."

Constable Malory nodded. "Aye, I'd come to a similar conclusion. I asked the fishing foremen to lend me some of their boys like they do in the summer, but they refused." With a sigh, he settled back into his chair. "I'm hoping they'll come around if you can add a few smaller victories to what you did yesterday, and get these cells filled."

"Let me guess, you and Fendig won't be coming with us for these victories."

He shook his head. "We will help as we can, but you must understand my primary duty is to maintain law and order within the town limits."

"Great."

Raedrick picked up the final report and scanned it quickly. "Did the wounded guard from this last attack pull through?"

Constable Malory shook his head. "Alas, no. He passed not long after we got him to town. The Guildsmen from the Healers' Circle tried their best, but they say he lost too much blood."

"That's too bad. What about the woman? Is she still in town?"

"Oh yes," replied the Constable. "And complaining every minute about it. She's holed up over at The Oarlock. Word is she tried to hire every coachman in town to drive her down to Calas, but none of them would take the job."

Julian felt his interest piqued. "How come?"

Malory shrugged. "Too dangerous." A sudden grin appeared on his face and he chuckled, adding, "'Course, I can think of two men offhand who said they were willing, except for her attitude."

Julian had a feeling he knew who the Constable was talking about. "Good looking?"

Again Malory shrugged. "They don't seem to have problems with the ladies…"

"Not the drivers, the woman!"

The Constable blinked, and flushed slightly. Clearing his throat, he nodded. "Yes, quite striking in fact."

Julian grinned. This was turning out to be his lucky day. Giving Raedrick a little punch in the shoulder, he said, "I think I know where we can get some help."

Chapter Ten

Magery

J ulian knocked on the door, making a firm staccato series of thumps against the wood. A muffled voice from within indicated the occupant would be with them in a minute, so he stepped back and waited. Beside him, Raedrick smirked slightly but said nothing.

A short while later, the door swung open, revealing the woman Julian met the night before in the taproom. She was, if possible, even more lovely than he recalled. Recognition flashed across her face as she saw him, and she frowned.

"You again. I thought I made myself clear last night: I don't want to be bothered by the likes of you."

Julian fought down a surge of irritation. "We're here on business, Mistress Klemins."

Her frown deepened as he spoke. "How do you know my name?"

Readrick interjected. "I'm Raedrick Baletier, Mistress

Klemins. This is…"

"Jules Hiddenstrap. We've met."

Julian ground his teeth in irritation. "Julian Hinderbrook."

"Oh, I'm sorry." She didn't sound like it, and from the sweetly innocent expression she wore, she sure didn't look it either. Silence hung awkwardly between the three of them for a moment.

Finally, Raedrick cleared his throat and got back to it. "We're working with Constable Malory, Mistress Klemins. He told us about your encounter while you were with the caravan that was attacked, and we wanted to ask you a few questions about it."

"Law men, huh?" she replied. "You don't look the type."

"That's because we're not."

She smirked. "Hired swords then. These yokels must really be getting desperate." With a sigh, she gestured for them to come into her room. "Fine, let's get this over with."

Room was inaccurate. She had a suite. A sitting room, larger than the room Julian and Raedrick shared, lay beyond the entrance. A couch and two padded chairs sat in a loose circle around a low table in the far end of the room, near a crackling fireplace. Two other doors led out, one on either side of the room. A taller table stood near the door with a decanter filled with dark red wine and several glasses resting on top. Next to the table stood a small shelf that was filled with books. Julian recognized several titles from one afternoon of liberty that he spent within a bookstore in Calas. He normally didn't have the money to indulge in many books, and a man in his position couldn't afford to get overly encumbered. But he had always enjoyed reading a good story, so he found himself envying the collection.

"Can I offer you anything?" she asked.

Julian shook his head.

"No thank you," replied Raedrick.

"Suit yourself." Taking a moment to fill a glass for herself, she moved over to the couch and sat down. Taking a sip of the wine, she smiled faintly and said, "What is it you want to know?"

"Mistress Klemins," Raedrick began.

"Melanie."

"Alright. Melanie, how much of the attack were you able to see?"

She looked at Raedrick as though he was daft. "All of it, of course. At least, all of it until I slipped away."

"So what did you..."

"There were thirty-five of them, ten with bows. They started shooting and the wagon drivers tried to make a run for it. At first it looked like we were going to get away, but we turned a corner to find they had felled a tree across the road, so the horses could not carry us onward if they wanted to." Melanie shrugged her shoulders. "You can imagine what happened after that."

"Thirty-five. That's a fairly precise number."

Melanie gave Raedrick a long-suffering look. "I have a very good memory," she replied.

"I'm sure," Julian said. He didn't try to keep the irony of her statement out of his tone at all. "So did you get a look at their leader?"

Melanie shook her head. "They were split up into three groups, and each of them had a leader. I couldn't even hazard a guess which of them, if any, had overall command."

"How did you escape?"

She shrugged. "When I need to be, I'm very good at not being seen."

"I've heard you mages have some tricks that can help with that."

Melanie made a soft tsking sound in response to Julian's statement. "You are mistaken. I'm not a mage. The Magestirium does not admit women as students."

Julian snorted. "After what you did last night, do you expect…"

"A simple carnival trick, nothing more." Melanie's tone was casual, dismissive. But her expression had become guarded and wary.

"Like hell. I've seen that trick, and I know how it's done. You didn't touch your drink at all, and you sure didn't have time to suck down anything else. And the only fire nearby was the candle in the center of the table. So you can claim not to be a mage, and maybe you didn't go to the Magestirium. But you learned a thing or two about magic somewhere."

Melanie was silent for a time, meeting Julian's gaze with a level stare of her own. Finally she shrugged and looked away. "I suppose it is hypothetically possible that a young lady might encounter a certified graduate of the Magestirium, that the two of them might fall in love, and that he might pass on what he'd learned to her despite the rules against it. But if such a thing were to happen, she would have to be very careful never to let her ability become common knowledge, because the Magestirium's wrath is legendary in its viciousness." She looked back at the two men, an unspoken plea in her eyes.

Julian and Raedrick exchanged glances. Everyone has secrets, it seems, Julian thought. He wouldn't want his betrayed any more than she wanted hers. He gave Raedrick a small nod, which the other man returned with a quick grin.

"Your secret is safe with us, Melanie," Raedrick said.

"Who said it was my secret?" she replied, but Julian could not mistake the gratitude in her eyes.

"One thing I don't understand," Raedrick added. "If such a hypothetical lady existed and she was in a situation where her traveling companions were attacked like you were, why wouldn't she try to help? Surely her companions would keep her secret in exchange for their lives."

Julian nodded. "Yeah, we saw the mages assigned to our division wreak some serious havoc in battle. Lightning from the sky, fireballs...it was impressive."

Melanie sniffed. "Well, speaking hypothetically, the sorts of things you're talking about require more than just waving your hands around. There are incantations to make and very specific gestures and stances that must be performed in time with the incantations. Also, there are material items that are used up in the spell. If the lady in question found herself in a situation similar to mine, she would have two problems. First, the only spells that could have conceivably helped take several minutes to cast and would have left her exposed to harm for the entire time. More importantly, though, the material components involved... Well, some of them are worth more than that entire caravan and all its contents. She would have been foolish to expend them under those circumstances."

Julian supposed he could understand Melanie's point, but at the same time... To figure the cost of her spell components against the lives of her companions struck him as particularly cold-blooded. But then, he thought about several decisions his officers had made on the battlefield. Decisions that he had understood even if he had not always completely approved of. They all came down to math: don't risk twenty men to rescue one who was probably dead, things like that. Was her decision all that different from theirs?

Raedrick spoke again. "You've made it more than clear you don't want to be here. So where were you going?"

"Away."

"Away from what?"

"Let's just say it was time to leave."

That was suitably vague. And not that dissimilar to the thought process that got them started on their own journey. Julian looked over at Raedrick and saw from his expression that he was thinking the same thing.

Raedrick continued, "Well, as long as these thugs have the passes blocked, you're stuck here, you know."

"That's been distressingly clear for days. But thank you for confirming the obvious."

"You know we're working to drive the brigands off," Julian interjected.

Melanie nodded. "I assumed as much."

"If the group that attacked you numbered thirty-five, there's probably at least forty to fifty total. Pretty long odds for the two of us. But if there was someone in town who had knowledge of magic and could even the odds a bit, that might make all the difference."

"What would be in it for this person?"

Raedrick replied before Julian could. "The satisfaction of helping people in need. And," he added as a smirk began to form on her lips, "freedom. Once the brigands are gone, there's nothing stopping you from going wherever it is you're planning to go."

Melanie pursed her lips in thought. Leaning back on her couch for a moment she considered the two men. Julian felt as though he was being weighed and measured under her gaze. Finally, she shrugged and nodded.

"I may be able to do something to help. What is your plan?"

Chapter Eleven

The Plan

That is the stupidest plan I've ever heard."

There was never any mystery where Constable Malory stood on an issue, that much was certain. Not that Julian necessarily disagreed on this particular point, but as far as he and Raedrick could tell after talking it over all afternoon, there was no other way to go if they wanted to find out more information about the brigands.

"What's so stupid about it?"

Julian almost snorted out a laugh at Raedrick's reply. He knew the plan's flaws exactly; hell, he was the one who envisioned the basic premise of the plan in the first place.

Constable Malory looked at Raedrick as if he were daft. "You want me to just release the man who attacked you, give him back his arms and equipment, and let him go back to his friends? Why, so he can wreak more havoc out there?"

They were talking in one of the booths in The Oarlock. They had picked one near the corner of the room, as far from the other patrons as possible. It wasn't that he didn't trust his fellow townsfolk, Malory had said, it was just that secrets get more difficult to keep up as more people learn them. So they kept a close but unobtrusive watch on the other patrons to ensure they weren't discussing sensitive topics in the open.

Raedrick shook his head as he responded to Constable Malory's question. "It wouldn't be some charity project. He's leverage..."

"Damn right he's leverage. And that's wasted if he makes it back safely and lets his boss know what pushovers we are."

"Actually," Julian added, "that's what we want. The easier they think the target is the less likely they'll expend a lot of resources to keep the pressure on. Why bother risking it if we're just going to fold anyway?"

"Near as I can tell, Farzal's pretty confident as it is."

"True, but if we're so scared of him that we release one of his men and make an example of the two guys who injured him and killed his companions..."

Constable Malory snorted again. "What, you want me to whip you or something?"

Raedrick shook his head. "Not for real. But you can put on a show of punishment or something. Then you release him and he rides out of town feeling smug and superior."

"And then we follow him back to his base camp," Julian added.

Constable Malory nodded slowly. "I understand, but it's still a dumb plan."

Julian opened his mouth to reply and so did Raedrick, but the Constable cut them off.

"There are too many things that can go wrong. And then we'll be without a prisoner and Farzal will think we're cowardly and incompetent."

"So what would you do with him?" asked Raedrick.

"Have a nice show trial and then hang him. Leave his head on a pike where Farzal's sure to find him and negotiate from a position of perceived strength."

Now *that* was stupid. "If you consider Farzal riding into town with his whole gang in a towering fury to be negotiating from a position of strength, who am I to dissuade you?"

Constable Malory looked taken aback for a moment. Then he flushed and nodded, the wind leaving his sails noticeably. "Hmm. Maybe that wouldn't be the best idea after all."

"So we're a go then. When are you going to release him?"

The Constable sighed and shook his head. "Tomorrow, I suppose. The mayor is not going to like this at all." With that, he slid out of the booth and stood up. He took a step away, then looked back over his shoulder at the two men. "This better work."

"This is just the first move in the game, Lucian. Trust us." Julian had to hand it to him, Raedrick could be smooth and reassuring when he needed to. Constable Malory sniffed, but Julian noticed he cracked a smile as he turned again and walked out of the Inn.

The door swung shut behind the Constable and Raedrick looked quizzically at Julian.

"Ok, you want to tell me how we're going to follow this guy across the grassland around here without him or his teammates noticing?"

"I've been thinking about that."

"I hope so, because I have also and I'm not coming up with anything."

"That's what we have Melanie for."

Raedrick's expression was almost comic in its lack of comprehension.

* * * * *

Melanie met them shortly before noon the next day on the outskirts of town. She was dressed down from when Julian last saw her. Her dress was simple enough to pass unnoticed in most situations, but a closer look revealed that it was divided for riding and was made from the finest material. It also accentuated her curves in a very pleasing way as she walked toward them.

"I wouldn't go there if I were you."

Julian glanced sideways to see Raedrick giving him a knowing look. "What do you mean?"

"I know that look. She's not someone you want to go down that road with."

"Yes, yes. We're in business together."

"That's not what I mean."

Julian didn't answer for a short while. He knew exactly what Raedrick meant, and pretty much agreed. That didn't mean he wanted to admit Raedrick was right. Finally, as Melanie reached their side, he said, "I know."

"What do you know, bumpkin?" Melanie asked, looking curiously between the two men.

Irritation welled up within him. Bumpkin? He almost told her off, and to hell with the plan. Almost. Instead, he took a deep breath to calm himself and replied, "This is a big risk. If your trick doesn't work…"

"It will. As long as you don't screw it up. So you better do exactly what I tell you to."

Raedrick cleared his throat. "Ok, are you going to explain what this master plan is now?"

Julian laughed, both at Raedrick's words and at the incredulous expression on Melanie's face.

"Really, you haven't figured it out yet?"

Raedrick shook his head.

"I thought you said he was clever," Melanie quipped to Julian, receiving a shrug in return. Rolling her eyes, she addressed Raedrick and spoke very slowly. "I'm going to use the same spell that I used to get away from the merchant caravan when it was attacked. The spell makes it very difficult for someone to notice a thing unless the person knows exactly what to look for and where to look for it."

"You're going to make us invisible?"

She shook her head. "That's actually impossible. It is more of a suggestion to the mind that encourages people to not notice or pay attention to what they see."

Raedrick whistled softly. "That's a neat trick. How long does it last?"

Melanie shrugged. "That depends on the spell caster and what she puts into it. Anywhere from a few minutes to several hours." Both Julian and Raedrick opened their mouths to reply. That was not going to work. But she raised a calming hand and added, "But I will use the extended incantations and the strongest components in this casting. That typically gets me six to eight hours' effect."

"That should be enough," Julian said.

"I hope," Raedrick added. Glancing up at the sun, he moved his lips for a moment.

Julian suppressed another chuckle. He would bet good money Raedrick was doing sums. He always had trouble with numbers, even the simple formulas used to convert the sun's angle in the sky to the time of day.

Finally, Raedrick nodded to himself and said, "Malory should be releasing our prisoner in a few minutes. We'd better get a move on."

Melanie nodded and, opening her satchel, withdrew a large leather-bound tome and a stoppered jar made from opaque glass. She placed the jar carefully on the ground and opened the tome. After leafing through it for a short time, she tapped her index finger on one particular page and nodded in satisfaction. "Here it is."

"What do we do?" Julian asked,

"Stay right there and don't move until I tell you," Melanie replied absently as her eyes scanned the page. After a moment, she closed the book and deposited it back into her satchel, then picked up the jar again.

Slowly, carefully, she worked the cork until, with a soft pop, it pulled free. Then she closed her eyes and stood still for a time, the jar pressed to her chest, as she breathed in and out in long, slow breaths. She began chanting softly. It was almost too quiet to hear at first, but quickly her chant became louder until she reached her normal speech level.

Then her eyes opened and she began to move. It was as if she was dancing with an invisible partner; her feet landed in precisely chosen places as she turned a circle in front of them. Her chanting continued, becoming more rhythmic, in time with her footsteps. She turned a circle again and her voice became louder. As she turned to face the men, one at a time, she reached into the jar and cast part of its contents into the air above their heads and those of their horses.

Dust of some sort, sparkling in the sunlight from small reflective pieces that were entrained in it, puffed around them and gradually settled onto their heads, shoulders, and torsos. Julian had to forcibly restrain the urge to dust himself off. Next to him, it looked like Raedrick was desperately trying to hold back a sneeze.

All at once, Melanie's chanting reached a loud climax.

Then she stopped and once again clutched the jar to her chest.

"It is done," she said in a somber, dramatic tone.

"That's it?" Julian asked. "I don't feel any different."

"You don't look any different either, more's the pity," Raedrick quipped.

Melanie rolled her eyes as she re-stoppered the jar. "Of course he doesn't," she said. "You're both under the spell, so you'll see each other normally. Other people, though…" She shook her head. "I cast the spell, and I have to concentrate to notice you two. But even that might not work if I didn't know for certain that you were there. Believe me, you are both quite un-noticeable." With a pronounced smirk, she added, "Which is, I suppose, not that big a change."

With that, she replaced the jar into her satchel and turned away. "Good luck. Try not to get killed."

"I don't know about you," Raedrick said after she walked out of earshot, "but I've never been so inspired."

Chapter Twelve

A Walk In The Grass

A quarter of an hour passed.

Julian sat in his saddle next to his friend and tried not to grow impatient. The Mayor and Constable Malory were supposed to have brought the prisoner out by now. Where were they? Just then, he began to think maybe Melanie was right, and the people in Lydelton were just a bunch of yokels. But then the sound of horse hooves clopping on flagstone drew his eye. Three men, one of them leading a saddled horse, were walking down the main street toward where Julian and Raedrick waited. At last!

They drew nearer and their conversation slowly became audible. "...terribly sorry about this. We cannot control what drifters who happen to pass through do. You understand?" The Mayor was good. He actually sounded nervous, terrified even. His voice dripped with sycophantic pleading. Julian hoped he was just acting.

The brigand wore a deep scowl, but his eyes glittered with contemptuous amusement. "Of course I understand, Mayor Brimly. But I can't guarantee Farzal will. Those two killed some of our brothers, and you gave them shelter here. That will cost you."

"But…" The Mayor wiped his brow as his eyes darted toward the brigand nervously. "We didn't know…"

The brigand snorted and turned his back to the Mayor. Holding out a commanding hand to Constable Malory, he said, "My horse?"

The Constable's face was a storm cloud, but he handed over the reins without comment. The brigand smirked, a distinctly unpleasant sight considering the scabbed-over scrapes on his cheek and chin, the swelling around his eyes and nose, and the broken teeth in his mouth. In spite of the man's smile, Julian felt a certain satisfaction in seeing the results of his kick.

The brigand mounted the horse and adjusted the reins. He took one last look at Mayor Brimly, who bobbed his head and wrung his hands nervously.

"You will remember to give Farzal our offer?"

The brigand shrugged. "I'll tell him. He'll say no, but I'll tell him."

"That's all we can ask."

The brigand snorted again and dug his heels into the flanks of his horse. She surged forward into a canter and quickly carried her rider away out of earshot.

"Laid it on a bit thick, didn't you?" Constable Malory said, disapproval plain in his tone.

"I hate this. I hate it." The Mayor mopped his brow again. You would think it was the height of summer, as much as he was sweating, Julian thought. The Mayor looked around, his frantic expression making it apparent he wasn't acting much at all. "Where are they?"

"They said they were going to follow at a distance and avoid being seen. They wouldn't wait right here for him."

Julian grinned and exchanged glances with Raedrick. He hadn't doubted Melanie's word, precisely, but it was nice to get confirmation that her spell had worked. Raedrick returned the grin and nodded toward the brigand, now several hundred yards away.

They kicked their horses into a fast trot and set off after the fleeing man.

* * * * *

The brigand slowed after a quarter mile or so. His horse could only canter so far, and it wasn't like she was a racehorse or battle-trained. Truth be told, Julian was surprised she went that far before having to walk. It was just as well, because he had no desire to waste his and Raedrick's horses to follow the thug.

For the rest of the afternoon, they followed about a tenth of a mile behind the brigand as he rode south. From their position behind him, he appeared wary, looking behind himself every few minutes. Julian couldn't blame him. The Mayor was clearly spooked, but Constable Malory hadn't even tried to pretend to be scared. Considering the brigand's line of work, treachery was probably second nature to him, so Julian was sure he more than expected the Constable to have some trap set.

An hour after leaving town, they reached the ford across the Eastflow, near the burned out farmhouse that had almost cost the brigand his life. The bastard didn't even give it a second glance. He did glance backwards again, though, while Julian and Raedrick were in the middle of their crossing.

"Stop!" Raedrick cried.

"What? Why?"

"The splashing."

"Sonofa…"

Julian reined in, bringing his horse to a quick halt. He hated to leave his steed with his hooves in the flowing, cold water for long, but Raedrick was right: their invisibility, or whatever it was, that Melanie had bestowed probably would not conceal the splashes from their crossing.

Were they blown already?

The brigand stopped also, looking back over his shoulder for a long few minutes. It was impossible to see his expression from that distance, but Julian imagined he wore a mask of concentration as he studied the ford. A sudden chill went down Julian's spine. The swirling of the current around the horses' legs was probably distinctly visible as well. He was just about ready to kick his horse forward, certain that they had been spotted, when the brigand shrugged and turned around again, then nudged his horse into motion.

Julian exhaled, letting out a breath that he didn't even realize he had been holding. "Let's get going," he said, and urged his horse forward.

They quickly exited the ford and rode up to the burned out farmhouse.

"We'd better stop," Julian said, "and rub down the horses. We don't want them getting cramps."

Raedrick nodded. "Not here, though. I don't want to look at this farm."

"Me neither."

The brigand turned to the left, veering southeast toward the hills leading to the mountains. They followed and soon found themselves riding over a small hillock. In the miniature valley between it and the next rise, they stopped and dismounted.

It took several minutes to dry the horses' legs and rub the circulation back into their feet. Julian grew more concerned by the minute as they worked. For one thing, the horses' lower legs were extremely cold. For another, the brigand was getting farther away every second. In this hilly terrain it would be very easy to lose him. Finally, he and Raedrick determined they had done the best they could for their mounts and got moving again.

They reached the top of the next rise, and Julian breathed a curse. The brigand was nowhere to be seen.

"He's got to be here somewhere," Raedrick said in a concerned tone.

"Let's give him a minute, hope he climbs a hill."

And so they sat. And sat. After ten minutes, there was still no sign of the brigand. Where was he?

"Could be he's sticking to the low areas between hills," Julian said.

"If that's true, we may never find him. Damnit."

"Let's head out and see."

The next hilltop revealed more rolling hills ahead that gradually got larger as they ran up to the mountains that ringed the Vale. But no brigand. They looked around carefully, then moved off again. The story was the same at the next rise as well. And the next.

The sun was beginning to sink lower on the eastern horizon and the shadows grew longer. As they crested yet another rise with no sign of their quarry, Julian reined in his horse and turned to look at his friend.

"Well what do you think?"

Raedrick shook his head and made a gesture of

hopelessness. "We'll lose the light soon, and there's no way we'll find him then." He punched his thigh with a clenched fist. "How the *hell* did we lose him?"

"We'd better get back to town. I don't want to spend the night out here. It's bloody cold."

Raedrick let out an extremely colorful curse, but he nodded in agreement. Without another word, they turned back and nudged their horses into a trot. With luck, they might make it back before full dark.

Chapter Thirteen

Restart

The barstool was hard, but that was the least of Julian's problems. His thigh hurt like no one's business from the afternoon's ride, but that wasn't his biggest problem either. His ears rang from the laughter of several burly fellows off of one of the fishing boats down at the docks, and his cheeks flushed with embarrassment. But that, too, wasn't his big problem.

A glass on the bar in front of him lay on its side, its dark contents spreading slowly across the top of the bar as they drained out. It was almost enough to make him cry.

"The winner!" shouted Horace as he raised the arm of the man next to Julian up over his head. Julian should have known Horace was a fishing man from his attire the first time they met. And being a fishing man, Julian also should have figured he could more than hold his liquor. And so could all of his fishing friends.

The winner grinned and shook his raised hand in the air in a clenched fist of victory, then turned toward Julian. "Pay up," he demanded in a slightly slurred voice.

Julian nodded and reached for his belt pouch. Or rather, he tried too. It took three attempts to get the laces untied, then another two to get the proper number of coins out. At least, he hoped they were the proper number; it was hard to remember what their bet actually had been.

"Here y'go," he said and held out the coins, which the winner snatched away quickly. What was that fellow's name again?

"You alright, boy?" Horace asked.

Julian waved him off. "Fine, jus' fine. I'm…" He wanted to say something else, but all that came out was a loud belch.

The fishing men around him burst out laughing again.

"Bugger me," he muttered and pushed himself away from the bar.

He must have pushed harder than he intended because he found himself stumbling backwards. The taproom swayed and spun around him, and he began to get a queasy sensation in the pit of his stomach. That wasn't good.

His grasping hands found the back of a chair, and he smiled in relief. He managed to maneuver himself around the chair and collapse down onto the unpadded seat with a sigh. The room instantly slowed down, and he was able to at least somewhat regain his equilibrium.

Water. He needed some water.

"Right here," Horace said, pushing a cup into his hand. How had he known what Julian needed?

That was a worry for another time. Right then, all Julian cared about was getting that water down his gullet. When he finally came up for air, he let out a great sigh. His head still spun and he was still a trifle queasy, but that was fading quickly and at least he was less thirsty.

"Thanks," he said.

"Pleasure's mine." Horace pulled a second chair around and sat down. "What's got you so wound up, boy?"

"Whacha talkin bout?"

"You don't normally tie one on this way."

Julian spluttered. "Hey now.. You don't know me tha well..."

Horace chuckled. "I know when a man can hold his liquor and when he's gone well past his limit."

Julian waved off his words with a dismissive gesture. "I'm fine."

"You can barely stand. Really. What's the problem?"

Julian looked away from the old fishing man and toward one of the fireplaces. Pushing down a surge of queasiness from the suddenness of the change in his field of view, he swallowed hard before replying. "My friend an' me... Wer helpin Malory with the attacks."

Horace's eyes narrowed. "That so?"

Nodding, Julian replied, "Ya. Thing is... There's what, fifty of um? If we knew where they were based, that'd be one thing, but..." He threw his hands out in an overly exaggerated gesture of helplessness that sent the last of his water flinging out of his cup and into the face of a passing waitress.

"HEY!" she exclaimed.

"Oh, I'm so sorry," Julian stammered as he stumbled to his feet. He had a handkerchief somewhere... Ah there it was. "Here...let me help."

Julian held the handkerchief out and tried to help sop up the water on her shirt. She screeched and pushed him away. He found himself stumbling backwards until he struck something solid. Looking back over his shoulder, his spirits sunk as he realized that the something solid was a large man with an unruly black beard who had just stumbled forward into his equally large friend, spilling both their drinks.

"Gents, I'm real sorry…" was all Julian was able to get out.

The bearded fellow growled as he spun around. Then, from out of nowhere, a very large fist struck Julian in the cheek and he saw stars. He didn't stumble; he toppled to the floor in a heap. There he lay for a long moment, tasting blood as he tried to figure out what the gaping hole he was staring into was. Finally it came to him: he was staring into his now empty cup, which lay on the floor beside his head.

"Stay down." The deep gravelly voice could only belong to the bearded fellow. It probably would have been smarter to do what the large man said. But Julian wasn't in the mood to listen to the smart thing. Anger and a bruised ego demanded he get up and trounce the man.

That was easier said than done, however. Julian got his hands below his torso and pushed himself up onto his hands and knees. But there he stopped as another wave of nausea swept over him. He swallowed again to avoid losing his dinner and took a deep breath. Then, equilibrium restored, he forced himself erect.

Or rather, he tried to. But as soon as his hands left the floor, he collapsed again. Undaunted, he tried a second time, with the same result.

Somewhere above himself, he heard voices but he could not make out the words. Then suddenly he felt hands on his upper arms and someone hauled him to his feet. Two someones, in fact. Looking slowly left and right, Julian saw that he was being supported by two of his new drinking buddies, one of them the fishing man who won the bet.

The two men guided him to a table and helped him into a chair, then set another cup of water in front of him. As he sat down, he looked back over his shoulder and saw Horace talking with the two large men. A waitress, a different one, came by and delivered drinks, which the men accepted. Then Horace clapped the bearded one on the shoulder and, with a friendly grin, turned and walked away from them toward Julian's table.

Horace's smile faded as he sat down across from Julian. "Those boys are touchy, and they drink top shelf liquor. You just cost me a fair amount of money."

"I didn't ask you to help."

Horace snorted. "Didn't need to did you?" Drawing a deep breath, he paused for a moment. Then, making a dismissive gesture, he said, "Don't think anything of it. Now," he leaned forward and clasped his hands together on top of the table, "you were sayin'?"

"Bad day today is all."

Horace did not reply; he just fixed Julian with a flat stare.

With a sigh, Julian explained what happened, how they failed in their pursuit of the prisoner. He almost found himself telling Horace about Melanie's role, but caught himself at the last moment and instead took a drink of water.

"Long story short, we're back to square one, except that now they know who we are. And they'll come looking for us. We're screwed."

"Hmmph. Your buddy agree with you on this?"

Julian shook his head. "No. Rae's never one to accept reality, even when it slaps him in the face."

"Funny thing about reality, boy. How you look at it changes what it is."

Maybe it was just the alcohol, but Julian couldn't make sense of what that was supposed to mean. Reality was, well, reality. It didn't change.

Horace chuckled softly. "From the look on your face, I

just lost you." He stood up suddenly. Walking around the table, he clapped Julian on the shoulder and said, "I'll explain in the morning. When your head's not full of mud."

He walked over to the bar and spoke with the bartender for a short time, making some gestures in Julian's direction. Then Horace left the inn. His fishing men friends left with him.

* * * * *

Julian awoke to sunlight streaming in through the window in his and Raedrick's room and instantly wished he hadn't opened his eyes. His head pounded and his mouth was so dry as to feel gravelly on his tongue. He felt more than a little queasy as well, and the bright light did not help matters one bit.

Pressing his palms to his forehead, Julian groaned softly and lay still for a long moment. This was not going to be a good day. He glanced aside to the other bed and was not surprised to find it empty. Raedrick almost never slept in. But then, they couldn't really afford to be late risers. Knowing that didn't make it any easier to sit up and swing his feet over the side of the bed. Or to stand, grab a towel, and shuffle across the hall to the privy and the baths for his morning routine.

A bath left him feeling slightly more human. And as he tromped down the stairs, the ache in his head helped him ignore the twinges of protest from his wounded thigh. Maybe a hangover was good for something, after all.

The taproom had more patrons than usual in the morning. Maybe it was just that it was later than he normally came down. He limped over to a table near the bar, scanning the crowd as he went. Raedrick was nowhere to be seen, but

Julian recognized several men who stood in a cluster at the bar: the fishing men from last night.

He ordered tea and the standard fish breakfast, then slouched forward at the table and rubbed at his temples with his fingertips, wishing he could rub the ache out.

Sooner than he expected, he heard footsteps approaching his table and looked up. But instead of the waitress with his tea, Horace stood there. His weathered features were rested and alert as though he hadn't been up well past midnight drinking with the younger men at the bar.

"Morning, boy. Looks like you could use some help."

Julian winced. "Not so loud, please."

Horace chuckled and sat down in the chair across from him. The old man reached inside his coat and pulled out a small vial. He set it on the table and pushed it across to Julian, saying, "When that tea gets here, put some of this into it. It'll do wonders for your head."

"Is that right." He picked up the vial and held it up to the light from the nearby window. Within was an orange-red fluid of some sort. "I've heard of plenty of hangover cures. Tried them all." He raised an eyebrow at Horace. "None of them work."

Horace leaned back in his chair and scratched at his chin. "You this cynical about everything?"

"I'm not cynical. I'm realistic."

"Sure," Horace replied with a snort. "Well, how's this for realistic." Leaning forward, he tapped at the top of the table with his index finger. "Me and my boys are going to help you and yer friend. Just call and we'll be there to put the fear of the Gods into those thugs."

Julian blinked in surprise and looked from Horace to the other fishing men. They numbered a dozen in all, all weathered from days out on the lake, all solid and strong.

And every one of them was watching him and Horace from across the room, wearing the resolved expressions of men ready for a hard day's work.

"I don't understand. Malory told us you were leery about lending a hand."

"That's just the management." Horace spat to one side as he said the word. "I'm head of the Guild, though. If I say we don't work so we can help you defend the town," he grinned and spread his hands, "we don't work. And ain't a damn thing management can do about it, unless they think they can man the boats themselves. Cause they sure won't find anyone else in these parts to do it. We'll see to that."

Julian's jaw dropped. "How…"

"'Course, if I were to do that, management might just decide running a fishing company is too much trouble, close up shop, take their money, and run." Crossing his arms over his chest, he continued, "Me and my boys can run the boats, but we don't have the money or the contacts with the merchants outside the Vale to make it worth a damn. So it's a balancing act. Management knows I can shut them down, but they know I'm buggered if I do."

"So you're saying…?"

"I'm saying, boy, that those men there," he jerked his thumb in the direction of his men at the bar, "volunteered to help you two out, and I got management to keep paying them while they do it."

Julian looked from the men at the bar to Horace in disbelief, and found himself speechless for a moment. Finally, he managed to say, "Horace, I don't know what to say. Thank you."

The old fishing man grinned. "Reality looks a bit different in the morning, don't it?"

Chapter Fourteen

New Blood

Raedrick walked into the taproom a bit before noon. Spotting Julian almost immediately, Raedrick strode quickly over to where he was chatting with the new recruits near the bar.

Breakfast had helped settle Julian's stomach, but Horace's hangover cure was as miraculous as he claimed. His headache reduced to a barely noticeable throb, he smiled cheerfully as his friend arrived. Raedrick's opening comment removed his smile quickly, however.

"Good to see you're up and about. I've just been at the Mayor's office."

That could not have been fun. "Was it bad?"

"You could say that. I thought sure he was going to pull his hair out. He's terrified, convinced that we've brought more harm than good already."

"Does he want us to leave then?"

Raedrick shook his head. "I offered, but he practically begged us to stay." He sighed. "I'm not sure he knows what he really wants, except for this whole episode to be over. So we still have a job."

"That's good, I suppose."

Raedrick shrugged, then looked past Julian to the fishing men. "Who are these guys?"

Julian grinned broadly. "My dear friend," he made a sweeping gesture as though he were a herald introducing an arriving dignitary, "may I introduce our army?"

Julian had thought the morning could not get any better. The confused expression on Raedrick's face proved him wrong. "What are you talking about?"

Julian laughed. "These fine fellows have pledged to help us against the brigands." Wagging a finger at his friend, he went on. "I keep telling you, staying up late and drinking with the locals always reaps benefits."

Raedrick's eyebrows rose high onto his forehead. He turned to regard the fishing men for a long moment, his veteran eyes taking their individual measures in a silent appraisal. Finally, he cleared his throat and said, "Have any of you ever used a sword?"

One hand went up, from a swarthy fellow in his middle years near the back of the group.

"A bow?"

Three more hands went up.

Raedrick rolled his eyes and gestured for Julian to follow him. The two friends moved several paces away. Raedrick spoke softly, even though it was all but certain they were out of earshot.

"What the hell good does it do us to have amateurs backing us up?"

Julian knew this was coming. "I've thought of that, Rae.

All these fellows are strong and know how to work hard. They can learn."

A soft snort was Raedrick's initial response. "It takes months to learn the sword to the point where you won't accidentally stab yourself in combat. We have days. Maybe a week or two."

"But the brigands don't know they can't fight, do they? They look impressive enough to help with any negotiations we may do."

"And when Farzal calls our bluff, then what?"

Julian shrugged. "The bow's a lot easier to learn than the sword. Long as they stay out of reach..." He spread his hands. What did Raedrick want? This was far from an ideal situation, and beggars couldn't be choosers.

He could tell Raedrick did not like the idea at all, but he also recognized the necessity of increasing their numbers. After a brief pause, he nodded acquiescence. As Raedrick moved back toward the group of fishing men, Julian heard him mumble, "Lambs to the slaughter," under his breath. He hoped his friend's assessment was wrong, even though he secretly shared it.

More loudly, Raedrick said, "Alright gentlemen, it's time to learn a new trade. Meet us at the Constable's office in a half hour. If you have anything that can pass for armor - a leather apron, gloves, boots - or any actual armor maybe passed down through the family, bring it. Same goes for weapons. Questions?"

Several of the men shook their heads, but all remained silent.

Raedrick nodded. "Alright. A half hour."

With that, the men quickly dispersed, exiting the inn alone or in groups of two or three. All moved with a purpose, with a serious demeanor. It was hard not to be impressed by their attitude, at least.

* * * * *

Constable Malory appeared surprised when Julian asked him for the use of his bows and swords.

"How many?"

"All of them."

His jaw dropped. "Why?"

Raedrick grinned at him. "We've got some new recruits. I don't suppose you have a place to shoot around here?"

Malory nodded. "Down this street, just past the edge of town. Fendig and I set up a few targets for practice away from where most people travel. Who are these recruits?"

Just then the swarthy man who had claimed knowledge of the sword walked into the office. Though Julian still had his doubts about him, the man had on a leather breastplate that looked at least passable and wore a curved sword with a hand-and-a-half hilt on his hip. He looked the part, at least.

"We're here," he reported, then he turned to go.

"Wait," Julian said. "What's your name?"

"Selam."

"Have the others come in and grab a bow and a sword, Selam."

The swordsman nodded and exited the building. Constable Malory shook his head in surprise.

"I didn't know he had a sword. Hell, I didn't know he knew anything besides knots, currents, and tides. He spends more time on the boats than anyone." Malory smirked slightly, then looked at the two friends and shook his head. "How on earth did you convince the Covington brothers to let their men off work?"

"I take it they own the fishing company?" Julian asked.

Malory nodded.

Julian grinned at him. "Don't need an in with the owners if you drink with the workers."

The fishing men began trouping in and collecting weapons. Grinning a bit more at Malory's renewed expression of confusion, Julian clapped him on the shoulder and followed the first pair of recruits out onto the street. It was time to figure out what they had to work with.

* * * * *

Three hours later, Julian's spirits were quite a bit lower.

Despite experience having taught him to expect poor performance from beginners, Horace's pledge of support combined with the fishing men's eager attitude conspired to make him forget that lesson. Julian thought sure they would be, if not skilled, at least passable.

It was a struggle to claim even that much.

Not that the entire group was a loss from the start. The men who earlier claimed experience with the bow all managed to get arrows downrange without difficulty, and even hit the targets a time or two. Everyone else, though... Julian winced just thinking about it. Most of the men had bandages on their forearms from their bowstrings. Almost all were quite a bit less enthusiastic than they had been at the beginning.

"They *did* make progress," Raedrick whispered into his ear.

"A little." More loudly, Julian said, "Alright, gentlemen. That was a good start. Obviously, we've got a fair bit of ground to cover before you'll be ready for combat. We'll meet here at sunrise every day to work on it, and we won't quit until sundown, except for lunch. Before you know it, you'll be hitting bulls-eyes with ease." He managed not to sound ironic as he said that last. He seriously doubted many of them would progress beyond merely competent. But that was all he needed them to be.

"Are we going to work the sword too?" asked one of the younger fishing men. Julian would have called him slender except for his bulging stomach; everything else about him was thin as a rail. He had been the closest to promising of any of the men who had no previous experience.

Julian shook his head. "Yes, but one thing at a time. Once you can get arrows downrange with some accuracy, we'll teach you how not to stab yourselves. But your default should be the bow. A sword is a lot more difficult, and we frankly won't have time to make you proficient with it."

The young man nodded, disappointment clear in his eyes.

Raedrick spoke up. "You're dismissed for the evening, gentlemen." The men nodded and began to disperse when Raedrick added, "Selam, Hiram, Rolf, and Gilroy, please remain for a moment."

The swordsman and the three practiced bowmen lingered as their fellows departed. Julian waited until the others were out of sight before addressing them.

"Since you have more practice than the others, we're going to lean heavily on you when the time comes. Are you up for it?"

Selam looked uncertain. "I'm no good with a bow." That was an understatement, from what Julian had seen this afternoon. However, Raedrick spent some time with him and walked away impressed with his swordsmanship. No mean trick, that.

"That's why you're going to teach these three the basics of the sword while Rae and I focus on the others."

Selam blinked in surprise, then grinned broadly and nodded. The look he gave the other three was almost predatory. Julian made a mental note to keep an eye on him.

"In that case, we'll…"

"Raedrick! Julian!" Fendig's voice sounded as though he was in a near-panic. What was he doing here?

Julian turned around just as the Deputy came to a halt and bent over, placing his hand on his knees and panting heavily. He was sweating as though he had just sprinted the entire distance from town.

"What's wrong, Fendig?" Raedrick asked.

Fendig coughed and took a deep breath, then forced himself to stand up straight. "Farzal," he managed between breaths. "He just rode into town with a bunch of his men. He's going to the Town Hall for the Mayor!"

"Bugger me," Julian breathed. "We're not ready for a showdown."

Raedrick nodded in agreement. "Let's hope it doesn't come down to that." Looking at the four remaining fishing men, he said, "You guys spread out on the street and be ready to cover us if it comes down to a fight."

The four newcomers swallowed hard and nodded. Only Selam looked truly calm; the others looked ready to jump out of their skin. Julian couldn't blame them. It was far too early in the game for this sort of confrontation. And him all but crippled, too! It was enough to put the notion of flight into his head for a moment.

Then he met Raedrick's eyes and saw the same dread that he felt, but it was suppressed beneath a steely resolve. If he didn't know Raedrick as well as he did, he would not have known he was anxious at all. But then, he always had been good at projecting calm.

The two friends exchanged nods, and Raedrick smiled thinly. "Let's get it done."

Loosening his sword in its scabbard, Julian set off at a trot toward Town Hall, trying his best to jog through the twinges from his thigh.

Chapter Fifteen

Diplomacy

Julian tried to shake off the shiver that always came when his adrenalin began to flow while also licking his lips in a vain attempt to wet a mouth that had suddenly gone dry. He had long since stopped trying to figure out how it was possible to be exhilarated and terrified at the same time; by this point in his life he had come to recognize both as a soldier's constant companions on the eve of battle. That he felt them now, as he and Raedrick hurried to follow Fendig to intercept Farzal with the four fishing men following, should not have been special at all.

Yet for some reason it felt different this time. Perhaps it was the eyes of various townsfolk, their expressions terrified beneath a facade of confident hope, following them as they rushed past. Or perhaps it was the protests from his injured thigh, reminding him that if the meeting did come to blows he was not equipped to make a good showing.

Regardless, when they rounded the corner and emerged onto Main Street near the Town Hall, Julian's heart was in his throat. Seeing twenty men on horseback, all armed with quality blades and wearing good thick leather breastplates with steel plates sewn on or, in a few cases, mail similar to what he and Raedrick wore, did not help the situation.

The Mayor, Constable Malory at his side, was standing on the steps of the Town Hall, his hands clasped in front of him as he clearly tried not to appear terrified. He was addressing a pale-complected man who couldn't have been much older than twenty-five, thirty at the absolute maximum. He had sandy blond hair and a lean, muscular body with very broad shoulders. A scar crossed his forehead from his right temple to the brow of his left eye, and he wore a mocking smile on his face.

Julian recognized him immediately.

"Son of a bitch," Raedrick murmured. He recognized the man also.

Very quickly they were within earshot, and it was clear Mayor Brimly was at a disadvantage. Hardly a surprise, considering. However, upon seeing them, and the fishing men behind them as they fanned out along the width of the street just as Julian and Raedrick had directed them to, the Mayor squared his jaw and stopped whatever he was saying.

The brigands noted their arrival as well. Though they looked disdainful, particularly as they regarded the fishing men, they nonetheless adjusted their formation to keep the new men in plain view. For his part, the blond fellow looked over everything Julian's and Raedrick's men did with a measuring eye. Julian noticed his smile slip somewhat as he studied the fishing men. He was no fool.

Then his eyes alighted on Julian and Raedrick, and he burst out laughing companionably. "Well, well. Baletier and

Hinderbrook. What brings you to this fine township?"

"I think you know what, Isenholf," Raedrick replied.

The blond man laughed again as he shook his head. "Name's Farzal now, Corporal." He looked from Raedrick to Julian and back quickly. "I assume you're to blame for the men I lost down at the falls."

Farzal did not phrase it as a question, so neither Julian nor Raedrick bothered to reply. He sniffed at their silence.

"I'll take that as a yes." He sighed and shook his head. "Now normally, I take the skin off a man who kills one of mine. But I'll tell you what. For old times' sake, I'll let that slide, just this once."

"Very kind of you," Julian quipped.

Farzal nodded. "It is."

"You obviously know each other." The Mayor's tone was confused.

Farzal laughed again. "Oh we know each other, all right. We're closer than brothers, aren't we, boys?"

"We *were*," Raedrick replied. Turning to address the Mayor, he continued. "We served together in the Army. He was a squad leader in the other platoon in our company."

Constable Malory's expression grew even more severe than it had been before as he processed Raedrick's words. If anything, the Mayor looked more worried than ever. Farzal ignored them, though, focusing his attention fully on Raedrick and Julian.

"And it looks like I was wrong about you two." His mocking grin returned as he spoke. "I thought you had swallowed the propaganda completely. But look at you now!"

Julian got a sinking feeling in his stomach. This was about to get ugly. Glancing aside at Raedrick, he could see that his friend had the same thought. If Farzal suspected...

"What are you talking about?" The Mayor's worry and

confusion was obvious from the trembling of his voice. His eyes flitted back and forth between Farzal and the two friends, and he mopped his brow with a trembling hand.

Farzal's grin only deepened as he looked at the Mayor. "They were no more released from their enlistment than I was. No one was to be released." Looking back at the Julian and Raedrick, he spat out, "You left of your own accord, didn't you? You deserted."

There it was, out in the open for all to hear. The sinking feeling became a cold lump of dread that radiated chills throughout Julian's entire body. There was no denying Farzal's accusation; it was the truth after all. In the long silence that followed, all eyes turned onto them. Julian felt the urge to run away, not out of fear but out of shame. The Constable's stare, the respectful look of a colleague earlier, now held contempt. The Mayor's was worse, because his face was that of a man who had abandoned hope for despair, and was ready to do violence to the one who had taken that hope. In this case, Julian was painfully aware that he was the one.

Farzal laughed again and turned his attention back to Mayor Brimly. "So those two were to be your mighty saviors, were they?" He shook his head and snorted. "Payment is due in two weeks. Don't be late."

He nodded and his men began turning their horses away. A trio set off down Main Street; two columns of five spread out to either side of the street and began moving at a slower pace. Outriders and flankers taking station, Farzal looked back at Julian and Raedrick briefly.

"You two boys really ought to think about joining up with me. The authorities won't treat you any better for trying to play hero here when they catch you. There's strength in numbers, my friends. We can make very good money together. You won't find a better deal this side of the grave."

"Not a chance," Raedrick replied, taking on the stern tone he saved for green men under his charge who were making trouble. "I'll make you a deal. Ride out of here now and don't come back, and we won't put you down like a dog."

Farzal looked, if possible, even more amused than he did before. As he rode away and the rest of his men followed, his laughter echoed in his wake.

Julian watched the brigands grow steadily smaller until, not long after they rode past the town limits, they turned to the right and rode out of view. Swallowing, he braced himself then looked back at the Mayor and Constable. Disbelief, disapproval, hope, despair, terror, anger…all those and more were contained in their expressions.

"I suppose you'd like an explanation," he said.

They both nodded. Mayor Brimly gestured toward the Town Hall. "In my office."

* * * * *

Mayor Brimly's office occupied most of the second floor of the Town Hall. Which wasn't saying much, considering the entire Town Hall took up less area than The Oarlock's taproom. Despite being small, it was well appointed, with ornately carved furniture made from darkly-stained wood, no doubt harvested from the forested hills north of town. The desk was particularly impressive, a massively constructed, ornately carved piece that had clearly been designed to intimidate people on the receiving end of its occupant's attention.

Julian certainly felt intimidated, or if not intimidated at least threatened and judged. It was only natural, considering. But he still didn't like it.

The Mayor sat in his chair and looked at them over

steepled fingers. Constable Malory, a grimly disapproving expression on his face, stood beside the desk with his arms crossed over his chest. The fingertips of his right hand drummed rapidly on the muscles of his left forearm as though from anxiety. He probably couldn't wait to put them in irons; local law enforcement often received generous compensation from the kingdom for capturing deserters.

As though he was reading Julian's mind, Mayor Brimly said, "Why should I not lock you both up right now?"

Raedrick replied, "We're helping you…"

"The hell you are. You've not made any progress; in fact, you've made things worse for us." The Mayor leaned forward in his chair and scowled. "Farzal raised his price, to, as he put it, compensate the families of the men he lost. The men you killed."

"Before we knew anything about what was going on here."

"So you say," Constable Malory interjected. "Why should I not think you've been playing us from the start? For all we know, you could be in league with him."

"How stupid do you think he is?" Julian asked.

"What are you talking about?"

Julian sighed. "If we were working together, why would he tell you about us?"

Malory blinked and scowled then nodded with obvious reluctance.

"Fine," said the Mayor. "That doesn't change the facts about you, does it? Why should I trust you at all?"

Julian and Raedrick shared a long look. Then Julian shrugged. "Tell them, Rae." Mayor Brimly knew most of it already. He might as well know it all.

Raedrick nodded. Julian could tell his friend was as reluctant as he was, but there was little choice in the matter at this point.

Drawing a deep breath, Raedrick began talking.

Chapter Sixteen

Lawful Orders

Raedrick's heartbeat filled his ears, the thudding so loud he almost couldn't hear the screams of wounded and dying men all around him. He paid neither sound any mind; his only focus was the man in front of him and the movement of the man's sword.

They had danced around each other for an eternity. Three passes and still neither had struck home with his weapon. Through the prism of his concentration, Raedrick felt a grudging respect for the man. He was the enemy, yes, and his nation had waged brutal war against Raedrick's homeland. But he was skilled and he fought with honor. It was hard not to appreciate that.

All around him, men on both sides of the battle had stopped their fighting. Those in the immediate vicinity formed a loose ring around him and his opponent. All eyes watched as though entranced; all enmity was forgotten before the spectacle of the mighty duel.

Flexing his fingers on the grip of his saber, Raedrick advanced slowly. The man circled to the left, and Raedrick pivoted to follow. He feinted upward, but pulled back from the true attack as the man simply countered, a lightning-fast cut at waist level that forced Raedrick to leap backwards to avoid having his guts spilled.

Landing lightly on the balls of his feet, he had to dodge aside immediately as the man followed his cut with a rising thrust toward Raedrick's chest. He barely avoided the tip of the man's sword by twisting his torso as he moved to the left, but he felt the blade tug at his mail for a heartbeat before he pulled clear. Slightly off balance, the only counter he could muster was a quick kick upward with the ball of his right foot.

A soft grunt accompanied the satisfying feeling of his boot striking the man's side, and the man stumbled. Grasping his side with his left hand, he fell to the ground.

Raedrick moved in, but again the man's reflexes nearly proved his better. Rolling onto his back, Raedrick's foe made a wide cut at ankle height, forcing Raedrick backward just long enough for the man to spring onto his feet in a single fluid move.

They paused for a moment, eyeing each other carefully. Raedrick's opponent removed his hand from his side and returned it to the hand-and-a-half hilt of his sword. Then he inclined his head, a gesture of respect that Raedrick returned in kind. Just because they were trying to kill each other didn't mean they couldn't be civilized, after all.

Then the man advanced. His blade flicked upward, then abruptly descended toward Raedrick's front knee. Nearly taken by the initial feint, Raedrick froze for half a heartbeat. Too late, he pivoted backwards, moving his front leg to the rear, but not before taking a deep cut to his thigh above his kneecap.

Grimacing at the flash of pain, and ignoring the cheers from several enemy soldiers as their fellow finally drew blood, Raedrick cut downward with his saber in time with his pivot. The razor-sharp edge of this weapon arced toward his opponent. The man's eyes widened and he pushed backward off the balls of his feet, his only defensive option with his blade still whistling downward in follow-through from his cut.

Blade and man both were a blur of motion that suddenly stilled. A fine spray of red flicked from the tip of Raedrick's saber, which was otherwise unstained. The man blinked and his jaw dropped open in bafflement as he raised his left hand to the side of his neck. As his fingers touched the skin of his throat, blood began flowing from the cut. At first it was a slow seep, then it became a spurting rush. The man's eyes widened and he stumbled backward a half-step.

Then his sword dropped from the suddenly limp fingers of his right hand and he fell to the ground in a heap.

A low sigh seemed to emanate from the enemy forces as Raedrick's foe fell. One and all, those nearby all wore expressions of stunned disbelief. As he watched, their fighting spirit seeped out of them, almost in time with the last of his opponent's lifeblood as it left the wound in his neck.

The momentary lull ended as Raedrick's comrades took up a loud, enthusiastic battle cry and surged forward, passing him on either side as they charged. The enemy fell back before their renewed onslaught. Entire platoons fell before anyone in the enemy camp tried to rally the troops, but by then it was too late. Inside of a half hour, the kingdom's army swept the field, leaving only a few of the enemy wounded alive to see the sunset.

* * * * *

"Besting the enemy army's champion in single combat, Corporal Baletier singlehandedly dealt a devastating blow to enemy morale, enabling our forces to win a decisive victory. Corporal Baletier's unflinching bravery, unrivaled skill at arms, and stalwart example reflected great credit upon himself and were in keeping with the highest principles of service to the Throne."

The Brigade's Executive Officer finished reading the citation as the Colonel pinned a medal, green and blue fabric separated by a strip of gold from which dangled two miniature crossed swords made of silver, onto the breast of Raedrick's dress uniform doublet.

"Congratulations, Corporal," he said.

"Thank you sir."

The Colonel returned his salute then turned to the assembled troops and led them in a round of applause. Raedrick stood at attention and tried not to blush at all the attention.

Soon enough, the official ceremony was over and Raedrick limped down from the podium. He was eager to get back to his tent and change into less formal and more comfortable attire. And for a bath and a good night's sleep, followed by a week of leave back in Calas. It wasn't often that a soldier could partake in such luxuries, but the High Command tended to pull out the stops after a great victory. And by any measure, yesterday's battle had been just that.

His squad intercepted him at the bottom of the stairs. The five men he knew best in the world clustered around him, offering their congratulations along with good-natured quips, then walked with him back to their tents. It was a slow journey, and not just because of his injury. Throughout the camp, men he knew by name, by face, or not at all stopped to wish him well. One and all, they wore the exuberant expression of men who had not just survived, but conquered, in the face of what they all thought going into it was almost certain death.

The mood at their Company's tents was more subdued though. Men were hurrying about, putting their gear in order as though getting ready for action instead of preparing to go on leave. What was going on?

The platoon Sergeant answered the question as soon as he saw Raedrick and his squad. "Leave's cancelled. We're heading out."

Raedrick's spirits, soaring high a moment ago, sank like a stone. "Where to?"

"The scouts uncovered an enemy outpost about twenty miles from here. We're to take it out."

* * * * *

The Company assembled on the crest of the hill overlooking the enemy outpost. To Raedrick, it didn't look like much more than a country village. It consisted of fifteen or twenty buildings clustered around a central green. There was a small encampment of some sort on the east side of town, halfway around the town from their hill. Maybe that was the target.

"Doesn't look like much, does it?" Hinderbrook said.

Raedrick looked sidelong at him and grunted. "The scouts say it's a key outpost. Is everyone else ready?"

Hinderbrook nodded.

"Good. You know the signal."

Little else needed to be said. The men in Raedrick's squad were well drilled at this point. Months in combat conditions had melded them into a team that was second to none. Sometimes, it almost seemed like they were reading each others' thoughts, the way they fought as a unit. It was a beautiful thing to see in action.

There was not long to wait. Maybe ten minutes later, the word passed down the line to make ready. Raedrick gripped his reins more tightly and forced down his growing anxiety. He needed to be cool and collected to lead his men correctly. It would be all the more important since he was not at his fighting best.

Then a whistle sounded from the center of the line and was picked up by the platoon leaders. Advance at a trot. Raedrick dug his heels into his horse's flanks and began to post in time with her steps.

Again into battle. Would there never be an end?

* * * * *

Where was the enemy?

Everywhere Raedrick looked, old men, women, and children fled before the Company's advance. But not a one of them had a weapon of any kind. Confusion reigned on the faces of his squad members as well. They had their weapons at the ready, but there was no one to use them on.

The scouts and intelligence people had fed them bad information before, but never this bad.

At the Platoon Leader's order, Raedrick veered away from the main column and led his men to investigate a collection of outbuildings. Eager to actually accomplish something, his men fanned out as they neared the buildings. Dismounting, they quickly kicked in all the doors and conducted a search.

Their faces when they returned were more confused and almost dejected.

"Just a few kids hiding out. Other than that, there's nothing here at all, Corporal," Laremy reported.

"Better bring the kids along so we can muster them with the others. We don't want them getting hurt by mistake."

"Right."

It took a few minutes to get the kids out of their hiding spot. In the end, Hilbredth had to sing a song to coax them out. He had a fine singing voice and a kind nature, so these sorts of things always seemed to fall on him. Soon enough, though, they were all formed up with the smaller kids riding ahead of them on their saddles and the bigger kids walking alongside.

They made for the town commons, or whatever the locals called the central green. Standard procedure was to muster civilians there, where they could be accounted for, while the unit finished its sweep. That had the dual affect of preventing surprises during the search and minimizing the chance of harming the civilians.

Suddenly a plume of smoke began to rise from the other side of the village. Then a second, and a third. Screams reached Raedrick's ears, coming from the direction of the Commons. What was going on? Raedrick reined in and turned to his men. They all looked as nervous and confused as he did.

"Let the kids down." Raedrick looked for the oldest of the children and pointed at him. "You there! Do you know a better hiding spot than those buildings we found you in?"

The youth nodded, his eyes wild with fright.

"You're in charge. Take the others and go there. Do not come out again until you see me come back and tap myself on my head with the flat of my sword. Do you understand?"

The youth nodded again and began herding the other children together. Seeing that he had things in hand, Raedrick turned to his men. "Let's go. Keep on the alert."

Weapons drawn, his squad charged into the village at a canter. More smoke plumes were rising now and the screams and shouts were louder than ever. Biting back a curse, Raedrick turned into the Commons.

And cursed out loud.

The Commons was a scene right out of a slaughterhouse. Everywhere he looked lay hacked civilian bodies. Soldiers, mounted or on foot, chased down fleeing people and cut them down without hesitation. Some unfortunate women did not get that mercy. Several had been stripped naked and were being raped by soldiers. On the far side of the Commons, a large group of civilians was being herded into a large building, the Town Hall maybe.

Sitting on their horses in the center of the Commons, the Company officers pointed and shouted orders.

"What in hell is going on here?" Raedrick demanded in a fury. Just then, the soldiers finished herding the civilians into the building. They then chained the doors shut and backed away.

The Company Commander, a grizzled older Captain, glanced at Raedrick and scowled. "New orders from High Command, Corporal. Scorched earth: take no prisoners and leave no support for the enemy. Send a message that continued resistance means death for everyone." Though his tone of voice was strong as always, his posture and expression said he was as troubled by this change as Raedrick was. That did not stop him from turning to the soldier leading the contingent who had just herded the civilians into the building and ordering, "Burn it."

The soldier looked a bit sick, but saluted and turned away

to carry out the order.

Was he serious? Raedrick barked, "No! Sir, we cannot do this!"

The Captain scowl became deeper. "We can, and we will. More specifically, you will. Private!" The soldier who received the order to burn the building turned, flaming torch in hand. The Captain gestured to Raedrick. "Turn the duty over, Private." To Raedrick, he said, "Burn it, Corporal. Do it now."

The Private handed the torch over, looking relieved to be rid of it. Unable to believe what was happening, Raedrick looked down at the torch in his hand, then back at the officers. Behind him, the members of his squad murmured amongst themselves. He knew they were as discontent as he was.

The officers noted his hesitation and turned their horses to face him. The Captain leaned forward and spoke in an even, cold tone. "Light the fire, Corporal, or I'll have you up on charges for disobeying a lawful order and hanged this very night, decoration or no."

Chapter Seventeen

Course Correction

Mayor Brimly sat back in his chair, stunned. Beside him, Constable Malory's expression had softened. He and the Mayor looked at each other for a long minute.

"We did not set out to desert. But when High Command gave those orders..." Raedrick shook his head. "I would not execute such an order. Nor would I order my men to."

"No. No, I imagine you could not."

"The rest of us in the squad left with him," Julian interjected. "Disobeying an order gets you the gallows. Not reporting a desertion gets you almost as bad. But weren't none of us who could stomach staying with the unit after that."

The Constable nodded slowly. "What about Farzal? Or...what was it you called him?"

"Isenholf," Raedrick replied with a sigh. "Theobald Isenholf."

"He was a rat from the beginning," Julian said, earning a look of reproach from Raedrick. "What? He was. You just didn't see it because you were a Squad Leader as well." Looking back at the Mayor, Julian went on. "He had a cruel streak, and took matters too far even before things began going downhill. Then the officers found out that he had been stealing. They were going to make an example of him, but he left before they had the chance. Took a few of his cronies with him."

"And now here they are," Mayor Brimly grumbled. Grunting, he stood up and turned around to look out his office window. "This town cannot survive under Farzal's domination. He'll drain us dry. And we do not have the resources or know-how to deal with him on our own." Taking a deep breath, he turned back around. "Very well. The job is still yours, if you will do it."

"Your Honor, I..." Constable Malory began.

"Would you have done differently in their place, Lucian?"

Malory took a moment in answering. He looked sidelong at Julian and Raedrick and frowned. Then, finally, he shook his head. "No, I suppose not. But still..."

"We can worry about the rest after this crisis has passed," Mayor Brimly replied.

Malory nodded, clearly not happy even if he did understand. For his part, Julian didn't much like the sound of that. The only thing he could think of that they had have to worry about later was turning them in, and damned if he was going to risk his life for them just to be repaid like that. He was just about to open his mouth and say that when the Mayor spoke up again.

"You understand the Constable and I are bound by oath and duty to turn in deserters that we come across. However, if you will rid us of these criminals, we will pretend we did not learn of your past. Are we agreed?"

Raedrick nodded and Julian followed suit.

"Very well then. I'll leave you to get on with it."

* * * * *

Julian and Raedrick descended the steps at the front of the Town Hall. Their men, waiting in the street at the foot of the stairs, perked up when they returned.

"Is everything alright?" asked Selam. He did not truly sound concerned.

"No problem. The Mayor is calm again at least."

Julian's words evoked chuckles from the fishing men.

"Brimly is high strung, that's for sure," Rolf quipped. "But he means well. Now what?"

That was the question, wasn't it? Julian looked to the east, where the sun was beginning to dip below the mountains. The day was about done.

"Change in plans, Julian," Raedrick said suddenly. "You're running the training on your own tomorrow. Rolf, Hiram, and Gilroy will assist."

"Say again?"

"Selam and I are going to take an excursion tonight, and I doubt we'll be back in time to meet the others in the morning."

Selam blinked in surprise. "Where are we going?"

Raedrick pointed toward the end of Main Street, where the brigands had turned right after leaving town. "Twenty men on horses leave a trail that should be easy to follow. We're going to find their hideout."

"But Rae, I…"

"You're still hurt, Julian. You'll slow us down, and you'll be a liability in a fight right now."

"Now hold on…"

"You know it's true, my friend."

Julian wanted to deny Raedrick's words, but he could not. Even going up and down stairs was a strain, and would be for a number of days yet. Reluctantly, Julian nodded.

Raedrick smiled and clapped him on the shoulder. "Don't worry. We'll leave a few of the scum for you to handle."

With that, he and Selam set off down the street. Julian couldn't help but chuckle at his friend's bravado. All the same, he felt a pang of something that felt disturbingly close to jealousy as he watched them depart.

* * * * *

Twilight was nearing its end as Julian stepped into the taproom. Even though he had been in the Vale for a number of days, he still found it strange how quickly night descended in the valley. He was just as happy to get indoors, since the night's chill was beginning to set in. That was one advantage to not going on Raedrick's excursion; it felt like it was going to be a cold one.

The taproom was more crowded than usual. Men sat at every bar stool, and most of the tables were taken. It took a moment of thinking before Julian realized why: tomorrow was Godsday. No work on Godsday, so there was no reason for people not to stay up a bit later than normal, and maybe indulge in a little extra fun. Molli was behind the bar this evening, a change from her usual routine. Lani was probably around somewhere too, but Julian couldn't see her anywhere.

Instead of lingering in the entryway, Julian decided to go say hi to Molli at the bar. She was always good for a chuckle, and maybe a discounted drink. But as he hobbled around a full table and barely avoided getting run down by a hurrying waitress, he spotted another lady he had not seen in a while. Melanie sat, alone as usual, in a table near the fireplace on the right.

Julian altered his course without thinking twice.

The lady mage, or whatever she wanted to call herself, noticed him coming long before he arrived beside her table. He chose to believe the little toss of her head came from happiness to see him rather than something else, but it was hard to not notice the way she rolled her eyes as he continued toward her table.

Well, they say if you want to get close to a woman it's better to get her dander up than to not cause any emotion in her at all. Julian had always seriously doubted how wise "they" really were about women, but just then he clung to that thought like a drowning man to a twig.

"Good evening, Melanie," Julian said.

"Why do you insist on bothering me, bumpkin? You and your friend got your help, so can you leave me alone, please?"

"Yes, well, about that. First, I'm not a bumpkin. I was born and raised a city boy, if you must know. Second..." Julian cleared his throat softly. "Our plan didn't turn out so well."

"No." If sarcasm were gold, she would be able to live like a queen for the rest of her life.

"No, really, it didn't. But we're moving on to plan B. There is a chance we'll need to ask for more help, though." She rolled her eyes again, her expression even more annoyed than it had been. "But that's not why I'm here."

"Then why are you here, city boy?"

He simply could not catch a break with her. "Well I'm on my own tonight. You clearly don't have any company." He put on his most winning smile and gestured toward an empty chair at her table. "Eating with company is always better than eating alone."

"Not always."

Feeling slapped across the face, Julian had to force the smile to not become a snarl. "Well if you're going to be rude about it..." He turned to leave.

He could hear the eye roll in her tone as she spoke to his back. "Oh sit down, Julian. Honestly, it's no wonder you men are always fighting duels and starting wars, as thin skinned as you are."

Julian had half a mind to just walk away, but looking back over his shoulder, he was struck by the color of her skin in the firelight and how the flames reflected off her eyes. She really was stunning. And so, against his better judgement and the commands of his ego, he sat down in the proffered chair.

And had no idea what to say next.

The silence had become almost unbearable when their waitress finally came by to ask for his order. Silently blessing the waitress for her timeliness, he looked questioningly at Melanie.

"I've already ordered."

Nodding, Julian said, "Ale. And to eat, fish and chips."

The waitress nodded and made a note on her tray, then hurried off toward the bar.

"You're a true gourmet."

Now it was Julian's turn to roll his eyes. "Really, do you have to mock everything I do?"

Melanie sipped at her drink and smiled innocently. "You make it very easy." He opened his mouth to protest, but she stopped him with a raised hand. "But I'll try to be more gentle."

How kind of her. He half-snorted, half-chuckled. "Thank you."

They were silent for another brief period, during which the waitress brought Julian's drink. He gulped down a mouthful of ale and relished the flavor for a moment.

"Which city?"

Swallowing another mouthful of ale, he quirked an eyebrow at Melanie. "Come again?"

"Which city are you from?"

"Oh." He set his tankard down and shrugged. "Taris, on the coast of the Tymor Sea."

"Very cosmopolitan."

Irritation welled up. It must have been visible on his face, because Melanie rolled her eyes again and said, "I'm serious. It's one hell of a lot more worldly a place to grow up than my little village."

"Really. And where was that?"

She shrugged. "It's called Vernon's Passing. Not even a one horse town, in the middle of nowhere. I got out of there as soon as I was able."

Julian supposed that explained a few things. "You've come a long way."

"You've no idea."

Chapter Eighteen

Skulking

As Raedrick expected, the twenty horses had indeed cut up the ground fairly well. He found it hard to believe that Isenholf - he could not bring himself to call the criminal by his assumed name - neglected to think about that. So he halfway expected to find the rear guard lying in wait somewhere on the trail.

But when he and Selam reached the Eastflow ford without incident, Raedrick began to rethink his assumption. Maybe Isenholf had not thought about the trail he left. Or worse, maybe he simply did not care. He had not bothered to hide his contempt, even of his former comrades in arms. He had always been cocky, but not sloppy.

"He must be very sure that his advantage is unassailable," Raedrick said to himself.

"Or he's just an ass," Selam offered.

Raedrick blinked in surprise. He had not realized he spoke

loudly enough to be heard. He shook his head and chuckled softly before replying. "Always has been."

Selam chuckled as well, and the two men exchanged grins.

They had opted against horses for the pursuit. For one thing, riders were easier to spot, and this night's excursion required stealth. For another thing, Selam did not own one. And Raedrick did not feel right about loaning out Julian's without asking. So instead they had taken a few minutes to retrieve warm cloaks from their rooms and wading boots from the fishing company's warehouse, then set out after the brigands as twilight was beginning to settle over the Vale.

Even with the wading boots, crossing the ford was uncomfortably frigid. Raedrick shuddered in sympathy for the horses who had to cross it and made a mental note to get a few extra cubes of sugar for his mare. She had earned it crossing this three times in the last few days.

It was full dark when they emerged from the ford and discarded their wading boots behind an outbuilding at the burned farm. "It's going to be tough following even this trail in the dark, you know," Selam noted.

"I know. The moon should be up soon; that will help." Raedrick glanced to the west toward where he expected the nearly full moon to rise and was gratified to see a faint glow on the horizon beyond the mountains. Any minute now.

Selam was right. Even after the moon rose above the mountains, it was slow going. It helped to have some notion as to where the trail would lead. And sure enough, at around the same place the prisoner had turned southeast the other day, this large group made the same turn. At least that was not just a ploy.

As before, the riders moved into the hills, climbing the first several and then descending into the small valleys between them. After doing that several times, Raedrick was beginning to become irritated; how did he and Julian lose that guy the other day if he had gone on like this?

The question answered itself a moment later. As they descended the back of yet another hill, the trail abruptly turned to the left, heading due east down the center of the valley between two hills. The valley continued a fair distance, slowly veering back to the south. About a quarter of a mile further on, as the curve of the valley brought the first hill out of sight, the hill to the left became rougher, more boulder-strewn. Then suddenly a cleft in the hillside came into view: a narrow chasm between adjoining hillsides that stretched east and slowly rose higher into the hills.

"I never heard of a formation like that in this part of the Vale," Selam said, sounding and looking surprised.

"There hasn't been a farmstead in a while. How often do people come out this way?"

The fishing man shrugged. "Not too often that I know of. But then, I don't know all the ins and outs around here."

Raedrick looked sidelong at him. "I didn't think you grew up here."

"What gave me away?"

"There don't seem to be very many trained swordsmen in this town." Raedrick chuckled and added, "And you drop your r's. Folks from here don't do that."

Selam frowned as he looked away from Raedrick and back toward the chasm. "Even with that moon, it will be hard to see anything in there."

Ignoring the change in topic, Raedrick glanced up at the moon, now almost directly overhead. "We won't get any better light until morning. Might as well get moving."

"I know. Just saying."

Sure enough, it was extremely dark within the chasm. The passage was narrow; maybe two people could ride side by side, but it would be uncomfortable. Also, it looked as though the walls of the chasm actually narrowed toward the top. That all resulted in very little light making it down to the floor where Raedrick and Selam walked.

Fortunately, the floor of the chasm was smooth and devoid of loose rocks. No doubt the brigands had cleared it out to make for easier passage. All the same, both men stumbled on occasion and their progress was very slow.

At one point, Raedrick looked back and was surprised to see that they had ascended a hundred feet or more. Glancing upwards, it did not look as though the chasm walls were much lower than they had been before. That meant the hills the chasm cut through were large indeed. He wracked his brain, trying to recall seeing any hills high enough to conceal a feature like this when he and Julian had been here in the daylight, and came up lacking. What was going on?

The chasm continued to rise for a several hundred yards, then abruptly came to an end. One moment, Raedrick and Selam were walking in near pitch blackness. The next, they stepped out into a large open area that appeared chiseled out of rock. Or at least, Raedrick surmised it was open. He couldn't see very far ahead, but there were no distinguishing features except behind them. Rather than rolling hills, sheer cliffs, a couple hundred feet tall, rose on either side of the chasm and stretched out in either direction as far as Raedrick could see in the gloom.

Raedrick blinked. It was only marginally less dark here than it had been in the chasm. Confused, he looked up to find the moon. And saw only darkness, along with what looked like a smoky mist not far above the top of the cliffs. There was not even a hint that the moon was in the sky.

"Where is the light coming from?"

"I was just wondering that," Raedrick replied. Selam was

quick on the uptake. He liked that. "I'm not sure what's going on here, Selam. Do you want to go back?"

The fishing man looked at Raedrick with offended eyes and shook his head. "Haven't found what we came for yet."

Raedrick grinned.

They moved forward, away from the chasm. The riders' trail was no longer visible, but there was no doubt which way they had gone. After a short while, Raedrick looked over his shoulder and felt a surge of dread. The cliffs were no longer visible. It was as if reality ended in a dark haze an indeterminate distance behind them.

"Stop, Selam."

The fishing man looked at Raedrick in confusion. Then he looked back also and his eyes widened. For the first time, Raedrick saw fear in his eyes. He was not sure his would not show the same thing.

They hurried back the way they came. After a moment, the cliffs, and the chasm opening, suddenly emerged from the gloom. Raedrick was surprised at how relieved he felt when that happened. He found himself letting out a breath he had not realized he had been holding.

"Well at least we can get back."

Selam snorted. "We can also get turned around completely without realizing it and lose our way."

Raedrick pursed his lips. He hadn't thought of that. "Isenholf's bunch must have a way to safely get back and forth. Maybe we missed something."

They went back to the chasm opening and spent several minutes looking carefully around. The cliff walls, the ground, the swirling mist above, nothing escaped their attention. There *had* to be a way for them to know how to get back.

It was Selam who found it, by chance. He stepped back

from the cliff face to look at the walls at a different angle. After a moment, he shook his head and threw up his hands. Raedrick bit back a curse and turned away. Maybe there was something inside the chasm itself…

"Raedrick!"

He spun around, his hand going to the grip of his saber. But Selam was alone, squatting down not far from where he had been looking up at the cliffs. He vigorously waved for Raedrick to come over. Once he reached Selam's side, Raedrick's spirits lifted.

Seen from the angle Selam took while squatting, there was a fine silver inlay in the rock floor. It outlined a path about as wide as four men walking abreast which stretched from the chasm exit, straight ahead for twenty yards. There it turned abruptly to the right and stretched away out of sight into the mist.

"We weren't going the right way at all," Selam said, a slight quaver in his voice.

"It's a good thing we turned back when we did. Good job."

Raedrick stood and found he could still see the path's outline. It was almost as if, having found it once, he was now allowed to see it completely. Allowed by whom was not clear, especially since there was no one else around. But he couldn't shake the feeling that it was designed thus, for some reason.

"Do we go on?" Selam sounded a bit less certain, less confident, than he had before when Raedrick asked that question.

Raedrick nodded. "Haven't found what we came for yet."

Selam chuckled.

Chapter Nineteen

Base Camp

It was difficult to determine how long Raedrick and Selam followed the path through the gloom. Without the moon overhead, Raedrick had only his own internal clock to figure the passage of time, and he knew well how imprecise that could be. Also, very soon after setting out, the cliffs again vanished from sight. Without a reference point, it soon became impossible to judge distance either. It was almost as if time had stopped and distance had lost its meaning. Even though he knew it to be an illusion, Raedrick still found that notion extremely uncomfortable to consider.

So he was relieved when, out of the gloom ahead, shapes appeared: two columns flanking an open doorway were set into a rock wall. At first, Raedrick thought the wall was just another part of the cliffs, but it was too smooth and not nearly as tall. The gloomy mist swirled the same distance above this wall as it had the cliffs, however. Very strange.

Biting back a yawn - it was well past midnight - Raedrick drew his saber and ran toward the column to the right of the doorway. The whole setup made the hair on the back of his neck stand up. It wasn't just the oddness of the place. Where were the sentries? He half expected arrows to begin raining down from atop the wall, but none came.

He reached the column and pressed flat against it. On the other side of the doorway, Selam had done the same. It was good that he hadn't needed to be ordered to do so; Raedrick was becoming more and more impressed with him as time went on.

And with his sword. This was the first time Raedrick had seen it unsheathed, and he found himself doing a double-take. The blade was standard length, but curved almost as much as Raedrick's saber. Its edge was sharpened on the convex side of the curve and on the last half-foot of the concave side just below the point. Nothing unusual there except that it was obviously high quality workmanship.

It was the flat of the blade that drew Raedrick's attention. Stylized symbols and designs were etched into the metal down the entire length of the blade: game animals, fantastic creatures, stars, the moon in its various phases, and all manner of strange letters and symbols that Raedrick did not recognize. Done poorly, such a collection of inscriptions would have been cluttered, awkward. Not so in this case. Every symbol or picture flowed flawlessly into the next so that the whole became a beautiful work of art that captured the eye and would not let go.

Selam noticed Raedrick's study and moved the blade so he could more readily examine it. "A family heirloom," he whispered, "It has been passed down from father to son for many generations."

"I can see why."

Selam teeth flashed in the gloom as he grinned.

Back to business. Raedrick slid around the column until he could just peek through the doorway. Again, Selam followed his lead without needing to be told.

There was not much to see at first glance. The path turned to the left beyond the doorway and sloped upward along the outside of another wall. Raedrick presumed it reached another level area above somewhere, but that was obscured by the gloom. For a moment, he wondered if it was more cheerful here in the daylight. Given the lack of moonlight, he would wager no. Talk about a depressing place to lair, if that were the case.

"I imagine we'll come upon some sign of them before much longer," Selam offered. "Sentries, horse pickets...something."

"You'd think. Keep alert."

Raedrick noted Selam's expression from the corner of his eye as he slipped through the doorway: the annoyed look of a man who has just been told the obvious.

The trail started out ascending at a shallow angle, but before long the grade increased and the climb became more difficult. Raedrick imagined it would be even more difficult on horseback. Maybe they made a practice of walking their horses from this point. The slope made for a good way to slow an assault, regardless.

After an indeterminable climb, shapes began to emerge from the gloom ahead and above. Squared off like blocks, it was hard to make out what they were for a long moment. Then he and Selam ascended a few more feet and the structures came clearly into view.

It was a gatehouse, complete with crenelated walls, a portcullis, and a thick wooden gate. And a pair of guards with torches on the battlements on either side of the gate.

"Cover!" Raedrick pressed against the wall and slowly edged his way backward down the trail until the torches and battlements were only just visible.

"That will be difficult to breach," Selam observed. "At least from this approach."

Raedrick nodded. "But are there any other approaches? I wouldn't want to try to find a different way through this place to find it, would you?"

"Not in this life."

Raedrick hesitated. This was, without a doubt, Isenholf's lair. But they only knew marginally more than they had before coming. He was loathe to leave without getting more information. Perhaps they could scale the wall... But no, it was shear and smooth, with hardly a seam between the stones it was built from.

It was useless. They had learned all they could this night. "It's time to go," he said with a sigh.

Selam nodded and began moving down the trail. With one last look up at the gatehouse, Raedrick followed.

* * * * *

They made better time going out than coming in. Partly because they knew the way already, but mostly because of relief. Raedrick was not about to admit it to Selam, but the thought of leaving the oppressive gloom of this place, wherever or whatever it was, lent extra speed to his stride.

Before long, they stood before the chasm opening in the side of the cliffs. Beside him, Raedrick heard Selam breathe a sigh.

"Not a moment too soon. This place makes me nervous."

Smirking, at his own cowardice in not admitting similar feelings more than anything else, Raedrick replied, "I know what you mean. Let's get out of…"

The sound of metal striking stone echoed down the chasm toward their ears, causing Raedrick to stop talking mid-thought. He froze, sudden anxiety flooding through him. Then, far down the chasm, as glow appeared. Flickering and bouncing, the glow could only be from a torch that someone was carrying.

"Son of a bitch," he breathed.

He and Selam exchanged glances and Raedrick was again impressed by the other man's calm. They exchanged nods, then darted to the cliff face beside the chasm mouth. Just as they had at the columns, Raedrick took the right and Selam the left, blades drawn. There they waited.

Slowly, more noises began to emanate from the chasm. Footsteps, metallic clinking, and voices. It was hard to make out the words at first, but before long, the conversation became more clear.

"…good take."

"Ya. Farzal was right again. Didn't even try to put up a fight."

A short pause followed, then the conversation continued.

"Ain't it s'posed to be brightening up in here? Sun came up a while ago."

A loud snort followed, along with mocking laughter.

"Things don't line up here, you know that."

"Whatever. It's unnatural, I tell you."

A general murmur of agreement followed.

Raedrick glanced across the mouth of the chasm toward Selam and held up four fingers. The other man nodded agreement: there were four distinct voices in the conversation. If they got the drop on the brigands, it should be an easy fight.

If.

Though maybe a minute passed, it felt like an eternity, waiting there. His heart rate increasing rapidly from tension, Raedrick took a deep breath. Then another. He forced himself, in spite of becoming more and more keyed up, to breath slowly and deliberately; he had found over the years doing that helped him to focus. It did not do anything for his nerves, though.

Just when Raedrick thought they were never going to show up, a pair of brigands stepped out of the chasm mouth walking side by side. They were armed and armored the same as the others Raedrick had seen so far, though they looked weary, with bags under their eyes. I probably look even worse, Raedrick thought with an inward smile.

The two brigands looked neither left nor right, but continued straight ahead on the trail. Raedrick met Selam's eyes a nodded.

The two men sprang into action as soon as the next pair of brigands stepped from the chasm. Raedrick darted in with a backhanded rising cut from his saber at the same time Selam attacked his foe. The brigands both wore nearly identical expressions of shock as they fell, spurting blood from their throats.

The first two brigands had just begun to turn around when Raedrick and Selam spun and advanced on them. Selam's man managed to duck beneath his cut and roll to the side away from him. Raedrick's man also had quick reflexes; he turned all the way around and had his sword half-drawn when Raedrick's cut reached him. Only luck saved his life. Raedrick's saber struck his sword on its blade just above the hilt, sending the brigand staggering backwards but leaving him otherwise unharmed.

Shrugging off the sounds of fighting to his right, Raedrick advanced, feinting low and then cutting high in an attempt to end the fight quickly. But his foe was skilled and recovered his equilibrium faster than Raedrick expected, leaping backward to avoid the true attack as he finished drawing his blade. Then he countered, a straight thrust that should have run Raedrick through his midsection.

Except that Raedrick was not there. He lunged far to the left, lowering his weight fully onto his left foot as the thrust passed harmlessly through the air where his torso used to be. Then he followed up with another backhanded cut.

The brigand screamed as Raedrick's saber cut through the tendons in the back of his right knee, and he fell to the ground. Desperate fear and agony contorted the brigand's face as Raedrick moved. an awkward attack to ward him off, but Raedrick simply stepped within his swing radius and grabbed his sword arm by the wrist.

"Please no," the brigand begged.

Then Raedrick's saber tip entered the hollow where his jaw met his neck. The brigand spasmed once and went limp.

Raedrick turned around to assist, but found Selam's foe already dead and the fishing man standing there calmly with his arms folded across his chest.

"Why do you toy with him?" Selam asked.

Taken aback, Raedrick was not sure how to respond at first. Bending over to wipe the blood off his saber using the brigand's cloak, he looked askance at Selam. "What do you mean?"

"You let him counter twice. You are skilled enough he should not have been able to counter at all. So…why do you toy with him?"

Raedrick had no answer.

Chapter Twenty

Rifts

Melanie whistled softly and leaned back in her chair.

Julian had never seen her so impressed. He and Raedrick sat in the couch across the coffee table from her. Raedrick had just finished telling the tale of his exploits the night before last. Her eyes had grown wider and wider the more he spoke.

"I've heard of this sort of thing."

"Oh?" Raedrick replied.

Melanie nodded. "Timon told me about it. It's called..."

"Timon?"

Melanie looked at Raedrick with the sort of expression Julian had seen teachers use with particularly dense students. "Remember the hypothetical mage I told you about?"

He nodded.

"If that had really happened, Timon would be the mage in question."

"Ah."

Melanie rolled her eyes and shook her head quickly. "As I was saying, Timon told me about it. It's called a trans-planar rift. It allows passage from our world to one of the higher planes of reality."

Higher planes of what? What the hell was she talking about? Looking over at Raedrick, Julian could see that he was just as confused as he was. That helped. A bit.

Melanie must have seen the confusion on their faces because she looked at the ceiling and sighed, then stood up. A small writing desk stood over by the window. She retrieved a pen and inkwell along with a piece of paper from the desk and returned to the coffee table.

"Look. The material world we live in is not the sum total of existence." She looked down her nose at the two of them, adding, "You should have learned this from your school teachers, or at least from your priests, at some point."

Raedrick nodded.

Julian spread his hands and shrugged. "Yeah the priests always used to talk about how the Gods live in the higher realms, or some such drivel. Didn't mean much to me."

To his surprise, Melanie smiled. "Or to me either, to be honest. When Timon explained this to me, I thought he was putting me on at first. But it turns out to be true." With a little shrug, Melanie looked down at the paper and drew a line on it. "Let's say this is our material world."

"The world is not two dimensional," Raedrick pointed out.

Melanie gave him a long-suffering look, making Raedrick shut his mouth and slouch back in the couch, looking chastened. Julian found himself grinning. She could be a handful, but he found himself admiring her more and more.

"If we assume our three dimensional world can be represented by this line," Melanie said in an annoyed tone, which Raedrick responded to with a nod, "we can also represent the other planes of existence with lines." She drew several more lines on the paper, some above the world line and some below. "All have their own rules. Some are very similar to ours and can be visited. Some are different enough that to enter them means instant death. A few are so dangerous that even opening a portal to them could destroy wide swaths of the material world."

"How do we know that?"

Melanie looked at Julian and shrugged. "Trial and error. From what I hear, members of the Magestirium have experimented with accessing the different planes for years. Centuries, maybe. And they aren't the only ones." Her eyebrows rose high on her forehead. "Do you remember the tale of Ciril Eremot?"

Julian nodded. Who hadn't heard that story? How the ancient kingdom had come to a sudden end, destroyed by the Gods in a fit of rage. How the kingdom's entire existence had been wiped away, leaving only a deep crater that was filled by the inrushing water from the world's oceans. Wait…

"Are you saying the Ciril Eremot was destroyed because someone there accessed one of these…places?"

Melanie nodded. Julian felt a chill go down his spine.

"A trans-planar rift is a junction between our material world," Melanie placed the pen on the material line and drew a second line connecting it with one of the other lines on the paper, "and one of the other planes. If the plane in question is habitable, people can go visit. It's tricky, but it can be done. Even more tricky, it is possible to establish a permanent connection to part of a nearby plane and then create a bubble, if you will, of the material world within it.

I'll wager that is what you and Selam encountered, Raedrick. It would explain why time was different there, as well as the strange perception you experienced."

"How…" Raedrick stopped and swallowed. He looked as confused, as disturbed, as Julian felt. "How is that sort of thing accomplished?"

Melanie shrugged. "I've never seen or heard the incantations for it. If Timon knew them, he did not share. He did say that only the most powerful mages, wielding the rarest of compounds, could create a trans-planar rift."

"Bugger me," Julian said. "That means Farzal…"

"Isenholf," Raedrick corrected.

"Whatever. That means he has a big-time mage on his side. And we're supposed to fight that how?"

Melanie looked askance at him.

"No offense, Melanie. I'm sure you're totally capable. But you just said you don't…"

"I know what I said. You did not listen."

"Sure I did. Only the most powerful mages can do this sort of thing."

"True, but you did not stop to consider the implications of that fact. When I say only the most powerful can do it, I mean less than a dozen men in the entire world."

"So?"

"So, everyone knows who those men are. And where they are. These are not the sorts of people who tend to associate with criminals. Or to go somewhere without people knowing about it."

Raedrick interjected, "Alright. So if it wasn't one of those famous mages, who could have made this place?"

"Could be it's been there for a long time and we just didn't know about it," Julian offered. "There are a lot of old ruins everywhere."

Melanie considered his words for a moment, then shook her head. "It's possible it was there before, but these aren't the sorts of things you can just walk into by mistake. Sometimes they are tied to an object of some kind, a focus for the magical energy. He would have to have obtained the precisely correct object linked to that particular rift, and then known the correct procedure to activate it, in order to access the rift."

Raedrick frowned. "That leaves us with the fact that he has help from a mage."

Melanie nodded.

"Hang on a second. You just said…"

"I said he wouldn't have help from one of those particular mages, Julian. If the rift was activated through an object, a large number of lesser mages could make it work."

"Could you?"

She did not answer immediately. Looking down at her sketches of the planes, she picked up her teacup and sipped it, a thoughtful and troubled expression on her face. Finally, she looked up at them.

"I'm not sure. If I found the exact procedures associated with the object…maybe."

Julian and Raedrick exchanged troubled looks. This just got better and better.

"That means that Isenholf's mage is probably more skilled than you are," Raedrick said. It was not a question.

Melanie nodded. "Looks like you're definitely going to need my help again."

"Told you so," Julian said with a broad grin. That earned him an annoyed look that turned, after a moment, into a small smile and a nod from her.

Raedrick looked between the two of them, a thoughtful expression on his face. "Well we have one advantage.

Isenholf probably doesn't know we found his lair."

"How's that?" Melanie asked. "You killed four of his men."

Raedrick nodded. "True. But Selam and I drug the bodies a few hundred yards into the mist, away from the trail to the fort, and cleaned up or covered as much of the blood as we could. So it's possible they just think those fellows deserted."

"You hope."

He nodded again. "Yes, I hope."

"Another advantage," Julian said. "With your adventure, that puts him down nine men. If he started out with forty…"

"Thirty-five," Melanie corrected.

"He probably did not send all his men to the raid on your caravan," Raedrick explained. "He probably had at least forty men at that point."

Melanie frowned, but nodded. Then her eyes opened wide. "He's taken twenty percent casualties in less than a week! That's got to have some of his men thinking about whether they want to keep doing this."

"Exactly. If we can whittle away at him a bit more, maybe we can force his hand, get him to do something foolish."

A sudden thought occurred to Julian. "Melanie, what would happen if the object controlling the rift were destroyed?"

She pursed her lips in thought for a moment. "Most likely the rift would close forever. Although, I suppose there's a chance of something more dramatic happening."

"So best case, whoever was in the rift at that point would be trapped. Is there any way they could come back?"

Melanie shook her head. "No. There are an infinite number of planes of existence. Even if a highly skilled mage consented to recreate the rift, to target the exact place on the exact plane where they were located without a guide of some kind would be all but impossible."

"Well that's it!" Julian bounded to his feet, unable to contain his excitement. "We don't need to worry about fighting all of them. We just need to find that object and…" He made a gesture like he was breaking a stick in two.

Raedrick's eyes widened. "You might be on to something there…"

"No."

Melanie's emphatic statement took the wind out of Julian's sails. He looked back at her in confusion. "Why not?"

"Any object chosen to be imbued with this sort of power would have to be extremely durable, for the reason you just stated. I doubt you could just simply break it. But even if you could…where is it?"

"I don't know. That's why we need to find it."

Raedrick sighed ruefully. "No, Julian, she's right. They've probably got it hidden in their fort. Or Isenholf keeps it on him. Or the mage does. Either way, we'd still end up having to fight our way through his men to get it."

Julian nodded reluctantly. He hated that they were right, but he couldn't deny it. It would come down to a pitched battle after all. Wait a minute. "Melanie, why can't you just, you know," he waved his hand around in a way that he hoped looked mystical, "bring the chasm down and block the rift that way?"

Raedrick rolled his eyes. "Really, Julian? She's not a God."

"Didn't say she was, Rae. But mages can do some impressive things."

Melanie replied, "Julian, while that is theoretically possible, it's not practical."

"How come?"

"Well for one thing, like I told you before, the incantations for a spell that would actually move the earth would take a couple hours and the components would likely cost more than this town." Julian blinked, his initial enthusiasm blunted by her response. It got worse as Melanie continued. "But more important than any of that...I don't know any spell that could do that."

"Rubbish. We saw the mages in the Army do things like that."

Melanie nodded. "I didn't say the spell doesn't exist. I said *I* don't know it."

Julian sighed. "Well maybe we could roll a bunch of rocks down manually. You know, get a bunch of men from the town to..."

"Julian." Raedrick was eyeing him in his patented 'stop being stupid' manner.

And he was right. There was no way they had get enough stones moved in to block up the chasm without the brigands noticing it somehow. Then they would just have a fight on their hands, and they were not ready to face all of Isenholf's brigands yet. So be it.

Julian sighed again. "Alright. Let's figure out how to whittle him down some more, then."

Chapter Twenty-One

Observation

Melanie met Raedrick and Julian after the morning's archery instruction, and they all walked to Constable Malory's office. Unlike the last few times Julian had been there, both Constable and Deputy were present. They sat in their respective desks looking over paperwork of some sort or other. For a town that was normally quiet, those two seemed to have a lot of paperwork.

Malory looked up as they walked in and nodded in greeting. "Gentlemen." Then his eyes widened and he smiled with what appeared to be pleasure. That was different. "And Mistress Klemins! To what do I owe this pleasure?"

"Have you been able to find the answer to that question from yesterday?" Raedrick asked.

The Constable frowned and made a non-committal gesture. "I'd rather we talk about it in private."

Melanie's lips compressed into a frown. If what Julian had observed from her so far was any indication, she was about to let fly. Raedrick beat her to it, though.

"Melanie is working with us now. You can talk freely with her."

Constable Malory blinked in surprise. "Oh? That is…surprising."

"I don't see why it should be, Mr. Malory," Melanie said cooly.

"Well it's just that…" Malory trailed off as Melanie's stare became more and more icy and her frown became a scowl. Apparently not a total fool, he cleared his throat and gestured toward Fendig. "We haven't learned much yet. Fendig's been on it."

Fendig coughed, looking uncomfortable as their gazes turned to him. "We have not received any reports of additional raids or robberies since Farzal met with the Mayor. Are you sure they had just attacked someone?"

Raedrick replied, "That's what they said. And they had enough money on them, so it certainly looked like it."

Fendig frowned and looked through his documents again. He shook his head, looking confused. "I don't know where the attack could have taken place, then. No one has reported any trouble at all."

"That is odd," Julian murmured.

Raedrick shrugged, however. "Well whatever. We'll figure it out eventually." Turning back to Malory, he cleared his throat. "We've been making better progress with our recruits than I expected. I think they're almost ready to take into action."

"Well that's good. What did you have in mind?"

"Now that we know the location of their base, we're going to deploy some of our men to keep an eye on them. Once we know their operating patterns well enough, we'll begin harassing them. If we hurt them enough, they may start thinking there are better places to be than here in Glimmer Vale."

Constable Malory did not look impressed. "No offense, but your last plan didn't work out very well. Why should this one turn out any differently?"

"Because this is not their plan, Mr. Malory, it is mine," Melanie said in her best, most condescending tone. Annoying as it was to be on the receiving end of that tone of voice, Julian had to admit it was effective.

The Constable blinked, looking defensive all of a sudden. "I appreciate that, Mistress Klemins, but…"

"Do you have a better idea, Constable?" asked Raedrick.

Malory thought about it for a moment, then shook his head with a shrug.

"In that case, we'd like your help.'

"Anything we can do."

* * * * *

Malory stomped his feet and hugged his arms tightly across his chest, rubbing his upper arms vigorously. It was bloody freezing. When he said anything we can do, he thought Baletier would ask him to help prepare defenses around town or something. Not sit out in the middle of nowhere all night and freeze his tail off.

He and one of Baletier's fishing men, Gilroy, were camped on a hilltop near a great crack in the hillside. Baletier and his friend called it a chasm, but that was a misnomer if ever Malory heard one. It was more a chimney than a chasm. But then, Baletier did not strike him as much of an outdoors man. Probably never tried his hand at climbing mountains, or he would have known the difference. There was no way that thirty to forty men were encamped in that little crack, so what in the hell was he doing here? He would bet two to one this was just some scheme to get him out of town so those two and their little trollop could do Gods know what-all without interference.

"This is a waste of time," he grumped.

Gilroy shook his head, looking at Malory with a mocking grin. "You didn't have to come, Constable."

Malory scowled. He didn't have to take that from a fishing man. He opened his mouth to retort, but stopped. "What are you doing, Gilroy?"

"Filling in a hole."

"I see that. Why? That's the second hole you've dug in the last ten minutes."

Gilroy spread his hands in an 'no idea' kind of way. "Just doin' what the lady told me."

"How's that?"

Gilroy stood and picked up a small bag that was sitting on the ground next to him. Fishing inside it, he pulled out a small object and held it out to Malory.

"She said to take these and bury them in a ring around our campsite. Wouldn't say why."

Malory accepted the object and turned it over in his fingers. It was just a small piece of rock, micah from the look of it, with a small engraving of a person crouched beneath a shelter of some kind on one side.

"What is this?"

"Don't know. She just said to bury them with the carving facing outward and we would be safe through the night."

Great. Superstitious nonsense. That was all he needed. It was bad enough the Mayor insisted on shackling him with that pair, but now they brought a bloody-minded woman into it with a bunch of silly notions. He shook his head vigorously.

"I'll have none of that foolishness. Rocks to keep us safe?" He snorted and tossed the rock off into the grass. "Safe from what?"

Gilroy gasped as Malory threw the rock away. "Sir, she said it was very important," he said, and he bounded off in search of it. How he thought to find it in the quickly fading light was beyond Malory.

"Get back here, Gilroy, you fool."

Gilroy hesitated. He looked back and forth between the grass and Malory, indecision on his face. Malory scowled and waved vigorously for him to come back. "Now, Gilroy!"

The fishing man looked one last time at the grass where the rock fell then nodded and walked back to camp, his eyes downcast. "She was very specific, Constable."

He snorted again. "Specifically foolish." Malory turned and stomped over to the edge of the hill. The last of the light was just about gone, but he could just make out the valley below, and the bottom of the chimney. Nothing moved down there. Nothing would all night either.

To hell with it. Damned it he was going to stay up all night for nothing. He threw himself down onto the ground and pulled a blanket over himself. "You've got the first watch," he growled to Gilroy, then he rolled over to go to sleep.

* * * * *

Gilroy ran. Despite the burning in his lungs from breathing the cold night air. Despite the crushing pain in his side and the wetness running down his hip and thigh. Despite the fatigue that made his legs feel like rubber. Despite every part of his body screaming at him to stop, to rest.

He ran because to not run was to die.

He couldn't hear his pursuers any more, but he knew they were back there, somewhere in the darkness. They had been on his tail for hours, it felt like. To think they had decided to stop chasing him now after all that time was foolhardy at best. So he kept on running.

They came just after midnight, as he was turning over the watch to the Constable. It had taken forever to wake him up, and then he had done nothing but grumble before finally getting up to take the watch. But then Gilroy figured that's why he had become Constable in the first place. He would have been kicked off even the slackest boat on the lake inside of a week. Until recently, there was not much for the Constable to do in the Vale except tell himself how important he was; Malory was custom-made for that sort of job.

Gilroy lay down and wished again that Raedrick and Julian had not forbidden fires. It was going to take forever to get to sleep in the cold, especially with Malory stomping around. Eventually, he managed to set aside his general discomfort and doze off.

The sound of a twig snapping startled him to wakefulness. Sitting upright, he ignored the rush of cold as his blanket fell off his body and looked around. Malory stood off to the side, closer to the edge of the chimney, looking down into the valley.

"Did you hear that?" Gilroy whispered as urgently as he dared.

Malory turned his head toward Gilroy and sniffed. "Go back to bed or I will."

"No really. I heard something."

Gilroy stood up. As he did, he heard a soft whistling, then something slammed into his side and sent him tumbling back to the ground. For a heartbeat there was no pain, only the shock of impact and an unusual feeling of pressure. Then that all gave way to agony. He heard himself cry out before he realized he was doing it. Anxiously grasping at his side, his hand came to rest on a long, thin piece of wood.

An arrow.

On the other side of the camp, Malory shouted an oath. Gilroy looked toward him and saw several dark shapes emerging from the undergrowth around the camp. They advanced on the Constable. He drew his sword and made an attempt at fighting back, but it was obvious he was not going to last long before they brought him down beneath the weight of their numbers.

In a panic, Gilroy clawed at the dirt, crawling away from the Constable and his attackers. He had to get away! He felt a flash of shame but forced it down. There was nothing he could do for Malory; he had to take his own life into consideration now.

Gilroy reached a small tree near the edge of the camp and, grabbing hold of the trunk, pulled himself to his feet. He almost collapsed again; every movement sent a new rush of pain from his wound. But he managed to keep his feet.

Leaning against the tree for a moment, he looked back and saw Malory pinned to the ground beneath a great bear of a man. Three others stood nearby, one of them grasping at his arm as though wounded. That was something at least.

"Tie him up," ordered the wounded one in an unexpectedly high tenor. "Where is the other one?"

"He went down over there..."

One of the others turned to point toward where Gilory had fallen and breathed a curse when he saw that Gilroy was no longer there.

"Find him, you fool," barked the leader.

Gilroy did not need any more encouragement. He turned and ran as fast as he could. Which, admittedly, was not very fast. Every step was new agony as the arrow wrenched in his wound. He became light-headed from the pain and exertion and from the knowledge that they would catch up to him any moment.

Yet somehow they did not, and he found himself still running, though in honesty it was more a slow, hunched jog than a run. At some point, he could hardly remember when, he had snapped the arrow off in the wound. It hurt enough that he actually passed out for a moment, but he managed to make better time without the shaft impeding the movement of his arms.

Gilroy managed to smile in spite of it all. There ahead of him, as the western sky began to lighten from the pre-dawn glow, he could just make out the Eastflow. He was almost home.

Chapter Twenty-Two

Repercussions

This is a disaster. A total disaster."

Julian looked over at Fendig and felt a surge of contempt. Ever since they received the news of what happened, he had been less than useless. He fidgeted, whined, and paced, but didn't actually contribute anything of use. It was clear why he was the Deputy and Malory the man in charge.

"Calm down, man," he said. "It's not as bad as all that. At least Gilroy made it back so we know what happened."

Fendig sniffed and turned away, clearly not encouraged at all. Julian just rolled his eyes.

"The real question is what to do now."

The Mayor did not look any more pleased than Fendig. And truth be told, Julian was upset as well, though he suspected not for the same reason they were. They cared about Malory, and that was fine. In Julian's mind the greater cause to be upset, angry even, was that the whole thing was preventable. If they had just set up the ring like Melanie told them to...

"Now you do your Mayor thing and keep everyone calm," Raedrick said, "We'll continue fortifying the town."

"That's it?"

Raedrick nodded. "That's it for now."

"What about the Constable?" Fendig demanded. "Those thugs have him. Who knows what they'll do?"

"What they'll do is question him vigorously," Julian began.

"You mean torture."

"Most likely. Then when they have learned all they think they can, they'll either kill him or send us a demand for ransom."

Fendig paled and he licked his lips. "K-kill him?"

"It's possible," Raedrick replied, looking askance at Julian. "But not likely. Isenholf knows Lydelton values him, so he is more valuable alive than dead. I'd expect a ransom demand." Looking at the Mayor, he put on an apologetic expression. "Looks like the payment due next week just got a bit bigger."

The Mayor sighed and slumped into his chair. "I suppose so." He barked out a half-laugh and shook his head. "Not that it matters. We don't have the funds to pay the original demand as it is."

"Leave that to us, remember?"

Mayor Brimly nodded.

* * * * *

"The Mayor's right, you know," Raedrick said as he and Julian left the Town Hall.

"About what?"

"We need to do something else besides fortify."

Julian shrugged. "Hiram and Rolf are good shots. The others are becoming decent. Why don't we just attack? We were going to in a few days anyway."

Raedrick shook his head. "They'd kill Malory for sure."

"And that will be his own damn fault. Bloody fool."

They turned into the stable yard of The Oarlock. The midday customers were beginning to roll in, from the look of things. Pleasant odors wafted from the open windows to the kitchen, reminding Julian that it had been a long time since breakfast. He picked up the pace toward the taproom door, but froze as Raedrick grabbed his arm. Julian turned around to tell him to let go, but his friend suddenly wore a deadly serious expression.

Moving a little bit closer, Raedrick spoke in a low tone of voice. "Maybe not. He and Gilroy had the first shift, and they lit no fire. Even with Melanie's concealment circle incomplete, don't you think it was awfully convenient that Isenholf's men showed up right then?"

Julian frowned. "He's not a fool. He probably has his men do sweeps every so often."

"Yes, but to find them so quickly? They could have been stationed on any one of a dozen hilltops nearby."

Julian saw where he was going, and did not like it one bit. "You think he's getting information from someone."

Raedrick nodded. "It's the only explanation that makes sense. Someone told him where to look for our scouts, and when."

"There's only a few people who knew the plan."

"I know."

Chapter Twenty-Three

To Catch A Rat

Fendig left the Constable's Office an hour before noon. That was not out of character, from what Julian had seen. But instead of turning right toward Main Street and the tavern where he normally took his lunch, he turned left toward the makeshift archery range at the edge of town.

"He knows there's a fight coming. Maybe he just wants some practice."

Julian snorted. "Fat chance. He could have joined us there every day for the last week."

Raedrick chuckled softly. "True. But give the man benefit of the doubt."

Benefit of the doubt was one thing, but that was not their purpose this afternoon. They were out to catch a rat. He and Raedrick were not making use of Melanie's concealing spell this time, just good old fashioned cover and concealment. They wanted to be able to confront him if their suspicions proved true, after all. So they crouched behind the door in the back of a shop that stood adjacent to the Constable's Office. As Fendig walked out of their field of view, then crept out and darted around the next building, then the next, to keep him in sight.

Sure enough, he did not turn into the archery range. Instead, he continued on into the grasslands east of town.

Cover became more difficult as they left town, so Raedrick and Julian let Fendig get further ahead of them. Fortunately, there were a few hillocks, bushes, and trees scattered here and there they could use for cover. A good thing, too, since Fendig occasionally looked backwards, clearly checking to see if he was being followed.

"Being awful cautious, isn't he? That says it all right there?"

"Not necessarily," Julian replied. "He could be meeting his mistress or something."

Raedrick gave him a look that just screamed, 'Are you serious'?

Julian just shrugged and smirked. "Hey, you never know."

Fendig continued on for a few miles until a large copse of trees came into view on a hilltop off to the southeast. He veered to the right, directly toward the copse, and picked up his pace. From time to time, he looked skyward at the position of the sun, but he no longer looked behind. Either he was convinced he was in the clear or he was pressed for time. Or both.

After a brief conversation, the two friends decided to risk being seen by closing the distance between themselves and Fendig. They set off at a jog, circling off to the side and following the rise and fall of the terrain toward the hilltop in question, being careful to keep the rise of a hill between

Fendig and themselves as long as they could, to avoid being seen. But eventually, they came to a point where there was no more cover between the copse and them, and they were forced to wait until Fendig entered the trees before sprinting to the copse themselves.

For a moment, Julian thought he had given them the slip. The copse was larger than it had appeared from the distance. It would not be difficult for him to slip out while they were looking for him within the trees. But then the sound of a branch breaking, followed by a loud thud and a muffled curse, issued from the undergrowth ahead.

Julian bit back a chuckle and exchanged a sardonic look with Raedrick, who looked just as amused, and relieved, as Julian felt.

Raedrick indicated, using hand signals, that they should separate and circle around Fendig. Julian nodded and moved slowly around to the left, being careful to disturb as little of the underbrush as possible. It would not do to give away his presence.

In reality, he need not have worried. Fendig shoved his way through the copse without bothering to try to be quiet. Julian shook his head in amusement. Fendig would never make it as a...

"Took you long enough."

Julian froze. The speaker's voice was deep and gravelly, and came from the area ahead of him and to the right, right around where Fendig was. Moving slowly, Julian tried to see who it was, but even without more than the buds of leaves on the plants' branches, there was too much undergrowth between him and them to make anything out.

"Sorry. It took longer than I thought to get away." That was Fendig. He sounded nervous, but not surprised, to be meeting the other man here.

It looked like Julian's suspicions were correct. Raedrick would owe him a drink after this. Smiling thinly, Julian cautiously moved forward until he reached a place where he could see what was going on.

Fendig stood facing three rough-looking men in a small clearing. They could only have been Isenholf's men. They wore the same leather and steel armor the others of his band wore and they had the shifty look of men who prey off others. No wonder Fendig looked about ready to jump out of his skin from nerves.

"So what do you have for us?" The man in the middle was the speaker. A few years older than the others, he had several visible scars on his head, neck, and arms. No doubt who the leader was here.

Fendig swallowed and looked around the area quickly, almost as though he was afraid to speak. Finally, he replied, "What did you do with the Constable?"

The brigand snorted. "What do you care? He's out of the picture, and now you're no longer the Deputy. That was what you wanted, isn't it?"

"Yes, but..." Fendig wrung his hands anxiously, then tried again. "I thought maybe you'd scare him off, discredit him. Not... you know."

All three men burst out in mocking laughter which lasted for almost a full minute. Wiping his eyes as he got himself under control, the leader shook his head. "Don't worry, little Constable. He's not dead." His grin turned positively vicious. "Not yet."

Fendig shrank back, his eyes growing wide.

The leader rolled his eyes and said, "What did you think was going to happen? Did you think we were going to just let them spy on us? Should we have just asked please, with sugar on top, stop doing that, and, by the way, please send us the Constable so our pal Fendig won't have to live with his condescension anymore?"

Fendig's gaze fell to the ground, and he shook his head. Clearly he was out of his depth. Scared, ashamed, guilt-ridden. Julian almost felt sorry for him. Almost.

Then the brigand leader pulled a small pouch off his belt and shook it. It jingled loudly; from the sound of things, it was full of coins. "Maybe this will help you feel better," the leader said. He tossed the pouch to Fendig, who caught it with a half-smile. The smile became a full-faced grin of avarice when Fendig looked inside the pouch at the coins.

Whatever temptation Julian had to feel sorry for him evaporated completely.

"What do you have for us today, Constable?" The brigand leader put special emphasis on the title, and Fendig's grin expanded a little bit.

"They're focusing on building defenses around the town," Fendig said. "I think the incident with their scouts has them a bit spooked."

"Is that right," said the brigand leader. It was not a question.

Fendig nodded quickly.

"Anything else?"

Fendig frowned and stood in silence for a time. Thumbing at his lip, he appeared uncertain as he pondered things. Then his eyes widened.

"Yes! There is one more thing. There is a woman working with them now."

"A woman?" The brigand leader looked surprised.

Fendig nodded. "The lone survivor of your attack on a merchant caravan in the pass, two weeks ago. For whatever reason, she is involved now. Though what she does, I could not say."

The brigand leader frowned, but did not say anything.

Fendig apparently took his silence for disapproval and swallowed hard. "I...I know she gave instructions to the scouts. The survivor said..."

"Survivor?"

Fendig blinked. "Yes. You took the Constable, but the other man made it back to town."

The brigand leader's grimace made Fendig go pale until he gestured for Fendig to continue.

"He...he said she told him to bury things to protect the campsite, but didn't say how they would. I'm not sure what that means. But she seems to have some authority with the two men the Mayor hired; they do what she says."

Julian had to stop himself from snorting. They did *not* take orders from Melanie!

The brigand leader had a different reaction entirely. His eyes grew wide when Fendig mentioned burying the stones. He glanced at his fellows, who had similar reactions, then returned his attention to Fendig.

"You need to get more information about this woman. Who is she? Where did she come from? Who does she spend time with? Every detail. Do you understand?"

Fending looked confused, but he nodded acquiescence.

"Good. Meet back here in three days. And you better have something useful to tell us."

Fendig swallowed. He looked as though he was going to say something more, but instead he just nodded and backed away until he was out of reach. Then he turned and hurried back the way he came, snapped twigs and branches with every step.

"That's bad news, Yosef," said the man to the brigand leader's right. after Fendig was out of earshot.

The leader, Yosef apparently, nodded, though he looked

uncertain. "Possibly."

The other brigand snorted. "Bollox. Just superstition from a woman who don't know no better."

"And the two heroes?" Yosef spat the last word in digust.

He snorted again. "The same. Only reason we know the difference is we've seen the real thing."

The leader shrugged as though conceding his comrade's point. "Regardless, Farzal will want to learn of this. Let's get back to base."

As they turned to leave, a branch moving on the far side of the clearing caught Julian's attention. Looking there more carefully, he saw Raedrick through the branches. He had a deadly serious expression on his face. Pointing at the three brigands, he made a quick cutting gesture in the air.

Julian nodded in reply. He agreed completely; those three did not need to return to give that report to Isenholf.

* * * * *

Fendig's expression when Julian and Raedrick pushed the leader of the three brigands ahead of them into the Constable's Office was priceless. Surprise morphed into recognition combined with irritation, which then changed into shock, followed by dread and, no doubt, the recognition that he had been caught. Fendig's eyes danced between them and their captive wildly and his jaw worked as though he was struggling to find words to say.

"Look what we found, Fendig," Julian said with a jolly grin. "Care to open up a cell for us?"

Fendig nodded quickly and pulled out the cell door keys, then led them back into the cell block.

"We caught this fellow and his two friends about four miles east of town. They attacked us on sight. Between that and their attire, they're Isenholf's men for sure."

Fendig nodded quickly. His hands trembled as he turned the key in the lock of the third cell door on the right. "Where are the others?" he asked, a noticeable tremble in his voice.

"Still out there." Raedrick made a vague gesture toward the east. "Scavengers need to eat, too."

Fendig paled. Gulping, he swung the cell door open and waited while Julian shoved the brigand inside. Then he moved quickly to slam the door shut and lock it. As he turned the key in the lock, Fendig avoided looking at the brigand, who was slowly collecting himself. Rubbing at his wrists where Julian had bound him, the brigand almost looked grateful to be in the cell and untied. Except for venomous look he directed at Julian and Raedrick, and the look of contempt he reserved for Fendig.

"Let me out of here, Constable, or you'll be sorry," the brigand growled.

Fendig blanched and turned away.

"Now, that sounds familiar, doesn't it, Rae?" Julian said.

Raedrick nodded and fixed Fendig with a piercing gaze. "The first thug we brought in said almost the same thing to you, Fendig."

"Well why shouldn't he? Until you guys came here, they pretty much had free rein. I expect he thought Malory and the Mayor would be too intimidated to keep him."

"He thought wrong."

The Brigand barked out a mocking laugh. "Wrong? They released him with apologies, didn't they?"

Raedrick favored him with a smirk. "Because we told them too, so we could follow him back to your hideout."

The brigand's eyes widened momentarily, his mocking grin slipping a bit. He glanced from Raedrick to Fendig and back and ran his tongue over his lips as though suddenly uncertain of himself. Julian couldn't help but chuckle.

Turning back to Fendig, Raedrick's smirk faded, replaced by a grim expression. "Of course, both he," he jerked his thumb toward the locked-up brigand, "and the first guy asked *you*, not Malory. Almost seemed like he knew you."

Fendig spluttered. "Preposterous! I introduced myself when you came in. And this guy knows they have Malory captive, so he can't be Constable anymore." His tone was affronted, but his expression was frightened. The little weasel knew he was caught but was trying to feed them a line anyway? He had more nerve than Julian thought.

Raedrick nodded slowly and pursed his lips in the way he did while considering something carefully. After a moment, he looked at Julian and gave a little shrug.

"Relax, Fendig," Julian said and he stepped forward to clap the deputy on the shoulder. "It's just that we've been thinking Isenholf must have a mole here in town. So we followed you this afternoon."

Fendig's eyes went wide and he tried to pull away. Too late, little man, Julian thought as he took a firm grip on the former Deputy's forearm and used his own momentum to twist the arm behind his back and slam him into the bars of the cell next to the brigand's.

"How long have you been feeding them information, you slimy little worm?" Julian growled into his ear.

Fendig cried out in a mixture of pain and despair. Tears welled up in his eyes, but he did not say anything. Next to him, the brigand's eyes grew even wider, then narrowed in chagrin. There would be no release for him. Not unless Isenholf emerged victorious. That had to look like long odds from where he was sitting.

Julian snatched the cell keys from Fendig's hand and tossed

them back to Raedrick, who proceeded to open the cell across the hall from the brigand.

As he pulled Fendig away from the bars and shoved him into his new cell, Julian quipped, "Enjoy your stay."

Chapter Twenty-Four

The Signal

A column of smoke rising from the south; that's what he was watching for, and there it was. Hiram knew it would be coming, but dreaded it. They had trained for nearly two weeks straight, and though he felt comfortable with his own marksmanship, he was far less confident in that of some of his fellows. As for the sword...he just hoped it wouldn't come down to that.

He sat on a rooftop near the edge of town. The Mayor, at Raedrick and Julian's behest, had convinced the house's owners, and the owners of the house across Main Street from his perch, to erect a platform up there, to facilitate keeping watch. And to aid in the defense of the town, if it came down to it.

Which it looked like it was about to. Fortunately for Hiram, the plan called for as many archers as possible to man the rooftop platforms, then pull up the ladders behind them.

He should be relatively safe from having to use his sword up there. Hopefully.

Hiram picked up the horn resting on the platform next to his water barrel and lifted it to his lips. Blowing into it, he blanched as all that came out was a little squeak. He hated the damn things. Wetting his lips, he took a deep breath and tried again.

The horn's call rang out strong and true. Down on the street below, every eye turned toward his position. The people stood motionless for a long moment. Hiram could practically see the thoughts churning in everyone's head. Is it for real? Is this another drill? Then a second horn sounded, from the platform across the street.

The people on the streets scattered, running as quickly as they could to the boats or to designated mustering points. It was pandemonium for a few minutes, then the streets became eerily silent, empty. That would change.

Hiram looked back to the south and his heart sank. The smoke column stopped abruptly. The smoke that was already in the air continued to rise, but no more rose to follow it. It was almost as if someone had taken a blanket and smothered the fire in an instant. He was not sure how that could be done, and he preferred not to think about it.

He just hoped the sentries at the Eastflow had managed to get away after lighting the signal. He was not intimate with the two men on duty this day; they were from different boats than he. But he had gotten to know them a bit over the couple weeks. They were good men, and it would be a shame to lose them.

A group came running from the center of town toward Hiram's position. He recognized Raedrick and Julian at the head of the group. Selam was close behind, along with half a dozen of his fellow fishing men, bows in hand. Strangely, that Klemins woman was with the group as well. Now that was a good looking woman. A bit uppity for Hiram's taste, but good looking regardless. Why was she there? A fight was no place for a lady like her, whether she was close with Raedrick and Julian or not.

Hiram was not sure what to make of those two. He and the others who had been with them to confront Farzal in front of Town Hall had heard the revelation about their background. They had not discussed it much, but Gilroy and Rolf did not care either way, and Selam...well, those two seemed to go up in Selam's estimation after that. But then, he had always been a strange fellow. But Hiram's father had raised him to value honor and to always do his duty. The thought of a man running out on his oaths by deserting the Army revolted him.

And yet...

And yet, Raedrick and Julian were stand-up guys. They did not have to stay here to help with the town's problems. Yet here they were, putting their butts on the line. It was hard not to respect that.

The group came to a halt on the street below Hiram's post and Raedrick shouted up to him, "Hiram, what do you see?"

"Smoke from the south, but it stopped all of a sudden."

Raedrick nodded with a frown and turned to the group. Speaking quickly, he issued orders that Hiram could not make out. Not that he needed to, since they all knew the drill.

Four of the bowmen split off from the group; two headed to Hiram's platform and two to the one across the street. Meanwhile, Julian, Selam, and the other two bowmen jogged to the end of Main Street, where workers had erected a makeshift barricade. To one side, an empty cart stood ready. The four men pushed it into the narrow opening in the barricade, then, working together, tipped the cart up on its side, effectively blocking passage.

The other two bowmen reached the top of the platform. Hiram turned to greet them and was surprised to see that Mistress Klemins had climbed up as well.

"My lady, what are you…"

"Doing?" she finished for him. "Nothing you would understand. Get back to keeping a lookout and don't worry yourself about things that don't concern you."

Well she did not need to be rude about it. Feeling more than a little affronted, Hiram was tempted to snipe back. Unfortunately, she was right. He had more important things to do than get into an argument with her. Instead, he re-verified the storage bins were full of arrows and then looked out to the southeast, where Farzal's men would most likely come from.

There was not much to see, though. And it was hard to maintain concentration with her chanting behind him. What was she doing? At one point, she even sprinkled him with dust of some sort. Him, and the other two men with him. And then the platform, too! He opened his mouth to protest, but the expression on her face made him bite his tongue.

Mistress Klemins finally stopped her chanting and climbed down the ladder. "Thank the Gods," Hiram breathed. That chanting was driving him crazy.

Then he realized there was a bit of a commotion in the street and the other platform. Men in both places were talking excitedly to each other, some of them with expressions of shock or fear. And they were pointing at him and his platform.

"What are they going on about?" he asked, receiving shrugs from the two men with him.

Then Mistress Klemins mounted the other platform and

performed her chant there as well, and he got his answer. No sooner did she stop chanting than the platform, and all the men on it, disappeared! His jaw dropped. Impossible! Rubbing his eyes did not help; they were gone.

Except he could still hear them. What the...

It came to him, and he looked down at Mistress Klemins in amazement. She was a mage! That was the only explanation for it!

"Nah. Women can't be mages," said one of his companions on the platform, as though responding to Hiram's thoughts.

"Apparently this one can," Hiram replied. He realized he was grinning, and the anxiety he had felt just moments ago was significantly lessened. With a mage on their side, they might just make it through this with their skins intact.

* * * * *

Raedrick nodded approval as the second archery platform vanished from sight. Or whatever it was that Melanie's spell did to make it appear to vanish. "That trick of hers never gets old, does it?" he quipped.

Julian grinned in response. "Yeah, she's right nice to have around."

Raedrick almost choked at that. Really? Julian must really be smitten. Raedrick did not think he would ever use the word nice to describe Melanie, however good to look at she might be. Although truth to tell, he preferred Lani in that way, too. Funny how that worked out. He had not thought about the fact that she would still be here when he decided to take the route through Glimmer Vale. He had only thought to get a good rate on a room for the night from Molli. And now he could not bear the thought of leaving Lani when this was all over.

But that was a thought for another time. For now, Raedrick spent the next several minutes looking over the barricade carefully. He was far from satisfied. It was ramshackle, obviously put together in a hurry, but that was to be expected. The best he could hope for was that it would delay Isenholf's men enough for the archers to drive them off. If not…

"I hope she has something with a little more firepower up her sleeve," he said as he turned back to face Julian.

And found himself facing Melanie as well. That was fast.

"I have a few other tricks, Raedrick. Fear not."

He nodded. "Fair enough. Hold off until I give the word, if you can. I'd like to keep you as a surprise for as long as possible."

She frowned, but nodded. "It will likely not be long. Once the archers begin to fire, their mage will put two and two together and take steps to find and counter them."

Raedrick did not want to think about what would happened when that started. "Can you handle him?"

Melanie looked at him like he was daft. "Do you have some information that I do not, Raedrick?"

"No. What…"

"Then you have just as much an idea how to answer that question as I do."

"Ah." He had no idea, and apparently she did not either. Wonderful.

"Riders approaching!" The shout came from above. It sounded like Hiram. Raedrick looked up and nodded, then did a double-take, as he was able to see his platform clearly. For a moment, anxiety welled up, far more than the normal pre-battle jitters he always felt. But then he moved his eyes slightly, and Hiram's platform faded from view again. It must be what Melanie said the first time: he knew it was there, so he could see it. If he worked at it, or surprised himself.

"Time to roll the dice."

Raedrick looked over his shoulder at Selam and nodded. The swarthy swordsman had a way with words, sometimes. Then he stepped up onto the small walkway that was constructed on the back of the barricade and looked out at the oncoming riders.

It was time to roll the dice indeed.

Chapter Twenty-Five

Fire And Blood

It was worse than he hoped for, but about what he expected. Julian counted thirty riders approaching. That meant that Isenholf had almost his entire force with him on this excursion, assuming he was not so stupid as to leave his base completely unmanned. And he was not.

Isenholf was taking this seriously, at least. His expression as he slowed his horse to a slow walk and approached the barricade was not the same mocking, amused smirk that he had worn before. Now his face was a mask of focus and malevolent intent.

Isenholf reined in, halting his horse about twenty feet from the barricade. He took a moment to look it over and made no effort to hide his disapproval. Behind him, his men arrayed themselves in a loose pack. All were armored as before. About half carried spears in addition to the swords on their hips. The rest carried bows. Except for one man at

Isenholf's right. He wore armor but carried no weapon that Julian could see. Instead, a number of bulging pouches hung from every place possible and he carried a thick leather tome balanced in front of him on his saddle. Unless Julian missed his guess, that would be the mage.

Isenholf completed his survey and turned his gaze on Raedrick and Julian. He nodded in greeting, a politeness that did not carry over to his expression or his tone.

"Baletier. Hinderbrook. You are becoming a true nuisance, do you know that?"

"That's why we're here," Julian replied, affecting a good-humored tone.

Isenholf's eyes narrowed a bit, but he did not acknowledge Julian's words. Instead addressing Raedrick, he said, "I have been more than patient. I gave you a chance, yet you continue to provoke me. Why?"

Raedrick shrugged and replied, "That's why we're here." He leaned forward and rested his forearms against the top of the barricade. "This town is closed to you, Theobald. You'll not get the money you want, so why don't you just go somewhere else? Somewhere with duller teeth?"

Isenholf snarled, showing his teeth. "Sharp teeth? Is that what you think you have with five men to defend your little wall?" Shaking his head, he went on, "No, I like it here. For the same reason you do: no authorities to come and check on things. A man can live on his own terms in a place like this. I think I'll stay."

"It appears we are at an impasse."

"Not at all. You can ride away right now, and I'll not chase you down." Isenholf paused for a moment, then added, "Last chance."

"Funny, I was just about to say the same thing to you."

Isenholf shook his head with a smirk, then turned away

and rode back to his men.

"Any second now," Julian said. They would just take a minute to get organized and then they would come. The barricade would not hold against their rush, and they knew it. He and Raedrick traded glances. His friend grinned and clasped hands with him.

"Ready?"

Julian nodded. "Let's do it."

Isneholf turned his horse around. His men gathered their reins. Those with bows nocked arrows. He opened his mouth to order the charge, but Raedrick beat him to it, simply thrusting a fist in the air and shouting, "LOOSE!"

Eight bowstrings snapped in unison: the six hidden on the platforms and the two behind the barricade. Six of Isenholf's men screamed and clutched at arrows that were suddenly lodged in their bodies; four fell to the ground, but the others stayed on their horses. Julian was actually impressed at the archers' accuracy.

Stunned surprise showed on every face in Isenholf's group. They froze for a crucial heartbeat, which allowed the archers to launch another volley before they scattered. Only three were struck this time, though it was not because of poor marksmanship. Two separate arrows flew toward the mage; both rebounded before striking him, as though they had struck a solid object.

A third of Isenholf's force was down or wounded. The rest darted for cover haphazardly. For a moment, Julian thought Lydelton might have an easy victory.

That hope was short-lived. Isenholf shouted, "Open it up," and the mage - the man had not moved a muscle despite the chaos around him - chanted a series of strange words at the top of his lungs and cast an object that he was holding toward the barricade. Julian could not make out what it was, but when it struck the overturned carriage, a tremendous sound, like a clap of thunder, rang out and the carriage launched backward as though kicked by a giant. It actually rose into the air for a time before falling onto the street and shattering about thirty feet behind the barricade.

Julian was stunned, as much by the noise as by the display of power. He had seen mages work their art before, on the front lines. But never from this close. It was impressive!

The others on the Lydelton side were apparently just as stunned as he, because no further arrows were launched for several seconds, allowing the brigands to surge forward toward the gap in the barricade.

Four men with spears led the charge, riding two by two through the gap. The two men in front threw their spears as they rode through, forcing the two bowmen on the barricade to duck to avoid being skewered. Then they were through, and there was no one to stop them from riding straight on to the center of town.

Except Melanie. She stood in the center of the street, her face the picture of calm, and regarded them with the contempt she would show a bug in her tea.

The brigands in the lead grinned viciously and drew their swords, then spurred their horses forward. In spite of his knowledge of her abilities, Julian felt a surge of panicked protectiveness. He hopped down from the barricade platform and drew his sword from his baldric. But even as he charged, he knew he would not make it in time to help her.

He needn't have bothered. Melanie tossed her head, sending her hair flailing around dramatically, and chanted three words while pushing toward the charging horsemen with outstretched hands. Something in her hands flashed into flame, but for a heartbeat that was all that happened.

Julian thought sure whatever she had tried failed, and she was about to be ridden down. Then abruptly the four horses screamed and reared, throwing off their riders, then fell to the ground themselves. The men hit the ground and screamed as well. Man and beast alike writhed in agony as bit, bridle, horseshoes, swords, breastplates, helms, belt buckles - everything made of metal - began to glow as though just removed from the forge. Flesh, clothing, and hair began to burn where it touched the white-hot metal pieces, and the air began to fill with the sickening smell of burning flesh. Within seconds, the charging quartet and their mounts were fully ablaze.

Two more brigands, who had followed the first quartet through the gap, pulled up short of their burning comrades, stunned horror on their faces. Arrows from the hidden archers slammed home, knocking them both from their saddles.

Reminding himself never to make Melanie truly angry, Julian turned away from the still screaming bonfire and hurried toward the gap in the barricade. More men would be coming through, and he needed to stop them.

Raedrick and Selam were already in the gap, each bracing a spear against the paving stones of the street; they no doubt retrieved the spears from where the brigands had thrown and missed. Another two horsemen tried to make it through, but were brought up short as the horses impaled themselves on the spears.

But throwing spears are not designed to hold up against the weight and momentum of a charging horse. The shafts cracked and then split completely, forcing Raedrick and Selam to dive aside to avoid being trampled. Julian heard Raedrick cry out in pain, but could not see what happened to him in the tussle of arms, legs, and bodies as the horses fell forward, sending their riders sprawling.

Julian rushed forward, cutting one of the fallen brigands down before he could extricate himself. The other was more nimble and met Julian with an attack of his own. Julian retreated, knocking the brigand's sword away as he gave himself more room to maneuver.

A sudden concussion from above drew his attention. The archery platform on the right side of the street blew apart. The men stationed there fell, grasping desperately at the shingles of the roof where the platform rested as they tried to slow or arrest their descent. One succeeded; Julian thought it was Hiram.

But he did not have time to find out for sure as his foe rushed forward, thrusting the tip of his sword toward Julian's gut. A sloppy attack. Even the fishing men, novices to the blade as they were, would not have tried it, but Julian supposed the brigand counted on his being distracted by the events on the roof to make it successful. Unfortunately for him, Julian sidestepped the thrust with ease and brought his blade down onto the back of the hapless man's neck. As the brigand's head went bouncing down the street, Julian thought he saw his last expression: a look of almost comic surprise.

Chapter Twenty-Six

Melee

Melanie noted with satisfaction Julian's expression, shocked and intimidated, as he turned away from her and rejoined the fray. He was charming enough, and certainly nice to look at, but it never hurt to keep a man off-balance. Besides, he, and Raedrick as well for that matter, seemed to forget sometimes that she was no delicate flower that needed protection.

Julian disappeared into the fray, and Melanie turned her attention elsewhere. The gap in the barricade was temporarily stopped by the corpses of a couple horses. Some of Farzal's men were climbing over on foot, though. Selam stood alone, sword in hand, to meet them. He could handle himself, from what she had been told.

The two archers on the barricade were having a rougher time of it. Three arrows flew over the wall for every pair they sent over. In retrospect, they probably should have stationed those two in the platforms...

The concussion of the right side platform's destruction drew her attention. She had been a bit surprised the other mage had not taken a greater hand in things yet, but apparently that was done. If he had seen through that platform's concealment, he would likely find the second one also. Unless she could defend that platform, their biggest advantage in this fight would be gone.

Drawing a deep breath, she opened her book. She had tabbed several pages last night, for quick reference. The third one dealt with incantations to repel hostile spells. She was familiar with them, and had practiced them many times over the last week, but it was vital to be precise, so she took a few seconds to glance through the text. It never hurt to check her memory one last time.

Satisfied, she pulled the necessary components from one of the pockets in her cloak and began the chant of protection. Silently, she prayed that she would not mess it up.

* * * * *

The first of the thieves climbed over the dead horses. Selam moved back a step to allow the man proper footing and give him a chance to ready himself. Honor dictated no less, and while these men may have tossed honor to the wind, Selam was not willing to debase himself that way.

Incomprehensibly, the thief looked surprised at Selam's gesture. How could a man fall so far as to not even realize what the dictates of propriety were? Grinning in what Selam presumed the thief intended to be an intimidating manner, he whipped his sword, a cheap-looking thing with too wide a blade to be practical, around in the air a few times. The fool should have just come for him instead of revealing how inept he was. He could not even flourish his blade properly!

Their encounter was over before the thief made his move. Selam could have taken him in his sleep; he had already shifted his focus to the next two coming across the horses when the thief made his completely predictable attempt at an attack and wound up skewered on Selam's sword instead.

Selam stepped forward and heard the thief stagger to his knees behind him, then fall over completely.

The two approaching thieves saw their ally's death and paused in their advance. They looked to each other for a moment then, reassured in each others' presence, moved toward Selam. They need not have been reassured; from the way they walked, their skills were no more impressive than their fellow. All the same, the two of them together were not to be dismissed as easily.

Selam stepped back again, out of politeness, and awaited their approach.

* * * * *

Beads of sweat budded on Melanie's brow and ran down her face. The strain of maintaining her concentration on the protective spell was getting worse. The other mage was strong. Very strong. She was not sure how much longer she could keep his attacks at bay.

Another attack came, stronger than the last several had been, and she staggered backwards. She almost lost her footing and her concentration.

Ahead of her, she noticed Selam squaring off against two of the brigands. Where were Julian and Raedrick? She had not seen them in some time. For that matter, the two archers from the barricade were gone as well. A chill went down her spine and she had to suppress a surge of panic. Was it just down to her and Selam, and the three men she was struggling to protect up on the platform?

* * * * *

The first of the pair of thieves fell beneath Selam's sword. He never stopped moving, dancing beneath the other's too-high cut and ending him as well with an upward slice of his blade.

Selam spun back to face the gap in the barricade before the second thief hit the ground. The area within the barricade was clear, for now.

"Selam."

The voice came from ahead, near the gap. He frowned and moved ahead cautiously. There, behind one of the dead horses. A hand was waving. Sprinting forward, low to make a poor target for an arrow or thrown spear, he reached the barricade and looked down.

And saw Raedrick lying beside him, his legs pinned beneath a horse. He managed to grin. "Took you long enough."

"Are you hurt?"

"Not badly, yet."

Selam grabbed Raedrick by the armpits and pulled him free. It was easier than he expected, making him surprised that Raedrick had not been able to free himself. But the angle was awkward; it would be more difficult for him alone.

Raedrick had just regained his feet when a great concussion from overhead announced the destruction of the second archery platform.

* * * * *

Julian parried an overhead blow from his foe and countered with a kick to the man's groin. His eyes bulged as Julian's boot made contact and he staggered backward. To his credit, he remained upright and kept his hands on the hilt of his sword instead of grasping at himself. But he was slow to react as Julian followed up the kick with his sword, and he fell in a heap at Julian's feet.

Four more of his comrades, and Isenholf himself, were drawing nearer. This was definitely not one of Julian's smartest moves ever.

He had felled his opponent and rushed to the barricade, ignoring the ache in his thigh which grew stronger with every passing moment. The wound had not yet fully healed, but sometimes you don't get to choose when you fight, so he had gritted his teeth and continued. At the barricade he met up with Willem and Gregor, the two archers. They were pinned down, but they saw one of their own, Tomi, who had fallen from the right-hand platform. Tomi had landed outside the barricade, but he was alive. For the moment. The brigands had not paid him any mind, but that could not last forever.

So naturally Julian came up with the idea to hop over the barricade with those two and rescue Tomi.

Like he thought as the five brigands approached, murder in their eyes: not his smartest move. Willem had an arrow through his upper arm and could not shoot. Gregor was as yet unharmed, but encumbered as he was dragging Tomi away, there was no way he could help. It was up to Julian alone, with support from the last archers in the platform, to hold the five off long enough for them to get Tomi to safety. Wonderful.

Then the other platform blew up, and whatever small hope Julian had blew up with it.

"Get him out of here," he shouted, and he backpedalled as

quickly as he could. The first of Isenholf's men got within sword length and attacked, but Julian avoided the cut easily. Then the second arrived, and he had to throw himself to the side to avoid being run through. Rolling to his feet, Julian spun around in time to catch another cut, from the first man again, with the flat of his blade. He pulled back again, dragging his blade down and to the side along the brigand's. He smiled as he felt the slight tug on his weapon caused by the tip of his sword cutting the brigand's right forearm.

The smile was short-lived, though, as the second and third men reached him again, flanking him on either side. No way to avoid this one. He gritted his teeth and prepared for the pain he knew was coming.

And was amazed when the brigand on his right stiffened and a sword tip exited the front of his chest. Raedrick's face appeared behind the man's shoulder. He winked at Julian and quipped, "Don't say I never did anything for you." Then he withdrew his saber and the man collapsed.

Needing no encouragement, Julian spun to his left and engaged the brigand standing there. His face, triumphal just a second before, now was a mask of dread as he fended off Julian's first cut. He countered, but Julian continued forward, not even bothering to block as he stepped within the circle of the brigand's swing. The hilt of his sword struck Julian's shoulder painfully, but more painful still was the stab wound that Julian's sword made as it entered the brigand's belly where the ribs met. The man coughed, spasmed, and slumped over, falling to the ground as he slowly slid off Julian's blade.

Chapter Twenty-Seven

Spellcraft

J ulian turned back around to find the other brigands down. Raedrick and Selam stood nearby, their curved blades red with the blood of many foes. Before them, only Isenholf stood. His pale face was streaked with blood from a cut over his left temple. It made a nice counterpoint to his other scar, really. He no longer wore his mocking expression. In fact, his eyes danced from Raedrick to Selam to Julian nervously. But he did not back down or lower his sword.

"The offer still stands, Theobald," Raedrick said across the intervening distance between them. "Ride away now, and we will not follow. You've lost a lot of men today, but you don't have to die as well."

Isenholf chuckled. "I have not yet played all my cards, Baletier." He cocked his head to the side and shouted, "Lorent!"

From off to the side, a deep, raspy voice replied, "Here, Farzal."

Julian turned his head and saw the new speaker. He instantly recognized him: the mage. He stepped from behind a jutting balcony that would have hidden him from the archers' lines of fire. With him were three more brigands. Two of them were dragging a man with a bag over his head between them.

The small group walked over to Isenholf's position and took up station just behind him. He smirked again and said, "Lower your arms. Or he dies."

The brigand with his hands free reached out and pulled the bag from atop the prisoner's head. Julian already knew who it was, but all the same his heart sank to see Constable Malory in that condition. He had obviously been beaten repeatedly. His nose was broken in more than one place. Both his eyes were black, his cheeks were swollen and he was bruised all over. It took a moment to recognize him, in truth.

But his eyes...

His eyes were fearful, tight with pain. Yet Julian saw a hint of iron within them that he never thought to see. An unwillingness to yield. From the look in his eyes, Malory seemed a totally different man than the Constable Julian had known. Stronger somehow. Which was exactly the opposite of what Julian would have expected, considering the torture he had endured at Isenholf's hand.

Looking back at Raedrick, Julian could tell that his friend was wavering, and he fully understood. Killing in battle or for justice was one thing. But for all his faults, Malory was a good man and did not deserve this. Julian could hear the thoughts going through Raedrick's head, because they were going through his as well. *How could I live with myself if I caused his death?*

But it all came down to numbers. Sometimes you did not risk those twenty men to save the one who was most likely dead already. And sometimes you don't sacrifice the wellbeing of hundreds in a town for one you happened to know personally. Julian opened his mouth to tell Raedrick this, but was surprised when Malory beat him to it.

"Don't do it," Malory called. "He'll kill me anyway, and then all of you…" His words ended in a pained grunt and a fit of coughing as the brigand who had removed the bag punched him in the belly.

"What's it going to be, Baletier?" Isenholf saw Raedrick's hesitation, and that mocking smile returned to his face.

Raedrick looked at Julian. He could see the conflict in his friends eyes. Slowly, Raedrick lowered his saber to his side and bent his knees. He was going to do it.

"NO!" shouted Malory, who had regained his breath. With a sudden jerk, he pulled his left arm free of the brigand on that side, then elbowed the man in the face. The brigand stumbled backwards, his hands grasping at his jaw where Malory's elbow impacted.

The Constable followed up with a roundhouse punch that caught the brigand who held his right arm in the nose. Even from where he stood, Julian heard the snap of breaking bone as that man also stumbled away. Malory righted himself…

And buckled over as the third brigand struck him again, this time in the chest. But unlike the last blow, he used a knife, not his fist. Malory coughed and a spray of blood flew from his mouth. His expression was one of disbelief as he fell to the ground, clutching at the wound that Julian knew would kill him in moments.

Raedrick halted midway to the ground. His eyes grew wide in outrage and, as Malory fell to the ground, a guttural roar issued from his lips. He heaved himself upwards and forward toward Isenholf, a murderous grimace on his face.

* * * * *

Melanie stepped through the gap in the barricade in time to see Constable Malory fall from the blow to his chest. She felt the sting of his wound as though it was her own; it made no difference that she hardly knew the man and thought him an incompetent fool.

As Raedrick, Julian, and Selam surged into action, the mage on Farzal's side began chanting a spell that Melanie recognized. It could freeze their muscles in place if he got the spell off, leaving them wide open to their foes. Without stopping to check her spellbook, Melanie immediately began the chant of protection that she had used to protect the archery platform. The fact that she had not been successful in her attempt at protection before never entered her mind.

* * * * *

Selam leaped to the side to avoid the thief's thrust. This was the first of the bunch who actually knew what he was doing. He and Selam had made two passes against each other, and each bore cuts as remembrances of the exchange.

He landed square on his feet and spun to face his foe. The thief was slightly off balance, the thrust having taken him farther than he probably expected when it did not meet Selam's flesh. He was wide open for the kill, but Selam stepped back a pace out of courtesy. Such a skilled foe should not be done in by a blow to the back.

To his right, Julian cut down another of the thieves, but received a cut to the meat of his shoulder from a second before he could spin out of the way. Further over, Raedrick and the lead thief faced off. Raedrick's dance was a beauty to behold. His foe was his equal in grace, if not in cunning, but the lead thief's greater strength seemed to be making up the difference. Had he the leisure, theirs was a duel that Selam would very much have enjoyed watching.

But his foe had regained his equilibrium and demanded his attention. The thief stepped to his right, circling cautiously as his eyes locked onto Selam's intently. Selam circled in the opposite direction, his easy movement on the balls of his feet keeping pace with the thief without difficulty.

It felt as though they circled each other for a long time, though Selam knew it had only been a few heartbeats. He was in no hurry to assume the offensive, though. He had taken the initiative on the first pass and nearly taken a mortal blow because of his miscalculation. He would not make that same mistake again, not against this man.

* * * * *

The pain of the cut to his shoulder flared counterpoint to the ever increasing ache in Julian's thigh. He backpedalled, evading a sweeping cut from his opponent by sheer speed of motion, and settled into a ready stance. He tried to flourish his sword, but could not do it properly with the wound to his shoulder.

So as his foe advanced again, Julian switched his sword to a left-handed grip and advanced to meet him with a cut from left to right. His left was not his preferred hand, but he had practiced fighting with it for just such an occasion.

The brigand's eyes widened in surprise as Julian's cut came from the opposite angle he was expecting, and it was his turn to backpedal. But he was not as quick as Julian; he escaped the attack, but his studded leather breastplate was cut clean through from nipple to nipple. The brigand staggered back a half-step, and Julian was gratified to see a slow seep of blood begin to ooze through the cut to the breastplate.

Julian grinned and flourished his blade, easing back into a stylized stance with his weight entirely on his right foot, his left only touching the ground with its toe, his sword parallel to the ground pointing at the brigand's throat, and his right hand above his head. The brigand swallowed and recovered himself, his movements a bit more ginger as he no doubt began to feel the stinging from his chest.

Julian winked at him.

* * * * *

At first Melanie was amused by the expression of shock on the other mage's face when his spell encountered her protective charm and he looked around to find her the only person not engaged in hand-to-hand combat. The notion that a woman had been the one to thwart him all this time was no doubt doubly infuriating. But his shock quickly turned to fury and he turned his full attention to her. Chanting an incantation that would stop her heart in her chest, he flung his hands out wide, casting a quantity of sulphur in her direction.

Desperation lent her swiftness as she shifted the focus of her protective chant from the men to herself. All the same, her chest constricted and she literally felt her heart skip a beat before the charm took effect. It was as though the weight of a dozen horses had been lifted from her chest. She breathed inward, feeling like it was the first breath she had ever taken.

But there was not time to rest. The other mage snarled and began chanting again. This chant was more complex, but she managed to beat him to the punch with a quick incantation of force which knocked him onto his backside. He yelped, his incantation ruined, and clambered to his feet again.

His face was a mask of fury as he began chanting again.

* * * * *

Selam felt satisfaction tinged with a shade of regret as his sword rose above his opponent's defenses and lifted his head from his shoulders. The thief's torso stumbled forward, completing the half-step he had begun before his death, then tumbled to the ground, spewing a small geyser of blood from the wound.

Selam stepped back, avoiding the body's fall, and bowed his head for a moment. He said a silent prayer for the dead thief's soul; he may not have been a man of honor, but his skill deserved a mention to the Gods. Maybe they would lessen his punishment in recognition of his ability. It was a small thing to hope for, but the notion of an artist like him languishing in never-ending torment caused Selam heartache for a moment.

The moment passed in the time it took for him to raise his head again and survey the field.

He saw Julian's foe fall beneath his blade, but Julian looked worn, battered. He limped toward Selam, and he was bleeding profusely from his shoulder. He would not be useful in battle for much longer, but his eyes were alight with the heat of bloodlust. He would drive himself to his death if he was not careful.

And no wonder. Selam turned to follow Julian's gaze and was once again entranced by the duel between Raedrick and Farzal. The two danced as smoothly as if they were a couple on the ballroom floor. Each thrust, cut, and parry was met by precisely the exact counter from the other as neither was able to make any headway.

Julian reached Selam's side and moved as though he intended to come to his friend's assistance. Selam reached out and grabbed Julian's arm, arresting his movement.

The young swordsman turned to look at Selam in confusion and anger. "Let go of me, Selam," he said in a low, dangerous tone.

Selam shook his head. "This contest is for Raedrick to win or lose on his own. You will dishonor him if you interfere now."

One of Julian's eyebrows quirked upward in confusion and he pulled away from Selam's grasp. He took a step forward, then stopped as he truly saw the duel for what it was. He slowly nodded and stood still to watch the drama unfold as the Gods intended.

Chapter Twenty-Eight

Showdown

There was no way Julian was going to be able to assist Raedrick against Isenholf, not without putting himself or his friend in greater danger. The two of them were too closely entwined, the duel too dynamic. He could step in and stab at Isenholf only to find Raedrick in the way of his sword before the blow fell.

So he stayed out of it, as Selam advised.

He had always been impressed with Raedrick's skill with the blade, but he had never seen Isenholf duel before. Silently thanking the Gods that it was not himself having to face their former comrade, Julian had to admit the other reason he did not step in to help. He knew just from watching that he was no match for Isenholf; he would fall before him within a single pass.

A concussion to the left drew his attention away. He felt as though he had been poleaxed when he saw what was happening over there.

Melanie and the mage stood about twenty feet apart, both chanting and executing the hand and body gestures of their art as rapidly as possible, to impressive effect. The source of the concussion that drew his attention was unclear, but a large plume of smoke rose from the ground not far from Melanie's feet. Her eyes were wide, with relief he thought, but she chanted on resolutely.

He glanced aside at Selam and saw that he was looking at the mages' duel now as well.

"You don't object to helping her do you?" Julian asked, with no intention of not helping whatever Selam said.

As he finished the question, Melanie completed her chant, and a ball of fire streaked across the distance between her and the brigand mage. It exploded upon reaching him, and for a moment Julian thought maybe she did not need help after all. But very quickly it became clear that while the fireball had engulfed the area around him, the mage himself was untouched.

Sneering, the mage finished his own chant and made a flicking gesture of his own. The grass between him and Melanie bent over, blown by a fierce gust of wind. Her eyes went even wider as the gust struck her, and she flew back against the wall of the building nearby. The wind left her lungs in a loud grunt of pain, and she slumped to the ground.

"I do not object," Selam said as he set off running toward the brigand mage.

Julian ran as hard as he could, slowly passing Selam toward the Mage as he willed his aching thigh to cooperate for just a few minutes more.

* * * * *

The magic-wielding thief stalked toward Mistress Klemins, a fiendishly delighted look in his eyes as he beheld her prone form. Selam did not hold much with the magical arts, by and large. They were a diversion for men without the strength, skill, and courage to face other men without prejudicial advantage. He recognized that magic had its occasional useful qualities; today's gambit with the archery platforms was one such bit of brilliance. Perhaps not completely honorable, but then neither was archery itself. But when faced with overwhelming odds, there is no dishonor in trying to level the playing field. All the same, useful things are not always things to be treasured, or held close. So it was with magic users, by and large.

But then there was Mistress Klemins herself. Beneath the cold and detached veneer she wore, Selam believed her to be among the most virtuous women he had met. It would not do to have the likes of her despoiled by a man such as this.

* * * * *

Melanie lay on the ground aching all over, and struggled to regain her breath. She knew the brigand mage would take advantage of her helplessness and tried to will herself to her feet. But her limbs would not respond for a long moment.

Finally, she managed to draw a deep breath and force herself to her knees. Looking up, her heart sank.

The brigand mage stood a few paces away, looking down at her with contempt. "You dare to challenge me, girl?" He spat the last word almost as a curse, his tone conveying all of the contempt for her gender that had been brewing within the Magestirium for centuries.

He flicked his fingers, and Melanie felt a force grasp her by the throat, force her to her feet, and pin her against the wall.

Grinning sadistically, he closed his hand slightly and she felt the force tighten around her neck, constricting her airway. She could hardly breathe!

The brigand's expression became more amused as he watched her struggle. "Where did you get…"

A body crashed into the brigand, knocking him to the ground in a tangle of arms and legs. Shocked, Melanie recognized Julian's profile and for a moment she felt relief. Then Julian cried out in surprise and pain, and he launched up into the air. For a second, he seemed to hang there, about ten feet up, then he crashed back down to the ground and lay still.

No!

She tried to force herself away from the wall, but the force held her fast. Its grip had lessened when the brigand fell, but not enough to break free. She managed to draw a deep breath though, and began chanting, desperately hoping she remembered the words to the counterspell incantation correctly.

* * * * *

The magic-wielding thief stood up and brushed himself off. He looked a bit disheveled but otherwise none the worse for wear from Julian's uncoordinated attack. Selam shook his head in chagrin at the man's foolishness. Stab or cut, do not tackle! The moment of surprise was lost, and Selam was sure the magic-user would not be caught unawares again.

Sure enough, the thief stopped abruptly, his eyes narrowing as he beheld Selam, who stopped in his tracks.

For a moment, the two men stared each other in the eye. The thief looked tired, and though he put on an air of confidence, he was afraid. Men always had a certain shadow in their eyes when fear had a grip on their souls. When that happened, dishonorable men could easily be induced to flee. There were many ways to accomplish that with a swordsman.

But Selam had never tried to spook a magic-user before.

* * * * *

Melanie watched as Selam advanced slowly toward the brigand mage. For a moment, she ceased her struggling against the force that held her fast, the sheer grace and economy of movement in his combat stride drawing her whole attention. He was not much to look at normally, but in this circumstance... He was in his natural element here on the battlefield, with his sword in his hands. That was obvious in the way he moved. Despite herself, in that moment Melanie couldn't help but think he was beautiful.

But that might just be because he was coming to her aid.

She shook herself, and was surprised and relieved to find she had continued the counterspell chant while her mind wandered. Timon's hard discipline while he taught her was paying off, it seemed. The chant was nearing its climax, and she would need the components soon: an ounce of wolfsbane and a sprinkle of copper powder. Blessing Timon's instruction to always have a hidden backup silently in her mind as she continued the chant, she shook her left arm vigorously - or as vigorously as she could in her constrained state - and a pouch that had been tucked up within her sleeve dropped into her hand. That pouch contained the components she needed; she had put it there on Timon's advice, given so many months ago.

She managed a smile as she continued chanting.

* * * * *

The magic-using thief backed away as Selam advanced. Fear showed more plainly in his expression; he was almost ready to break.

Then the thief surprised him. He made a raising gesture with his hands and from the ground around him several arrows and a pair of spears lifted up into the air. Stopping at waist level, the missiles all turned to point at Selam.

The thief smiled, a sadistic grin of triumph. Then, with a flick of his fingers, the first of the missiles hurtled forward.

* * * * *

Melanie's heart sank. Though she chanted as quickly as she could, there was too much of the counterspell incantation remaining for her to stop the brigand mage. His incantation was complete, and so long as he maintained his concentration, he would be able to do as he willed with force. She was actually halfway surprised he didn't just bind Selam as he had done her. He must be nearing his limit. Not that it mattered; arrows and spears would be more than enough.

Selam was doomed.

The arrow streaked toward him and Melanie cringed inwardly. Then she nearly lost her place in the incantation from shock as Selam, with a seemingly minuscule flick of his sword, knocked the arrow off course. It passed him harmlessly by and he continued to advance.

How did he do that? She had never heard of such a thing. A glance at the other mage showed he was just as shocked as she.

The brigand mage backed away a half-step and, with a flicking gesture of his hand, launched another arrow toward

Selam. But he spun away at the last second with only a tear in his sleeve to show for it.

Another arrow. Then another. And another. Selam avoided them all, receiving only minor scrapes and cuts. Melanie had never seen such grace! Still he advanced, and still the mage retreated and circled to his left to keep as much distance from Selam as he could.

The last of the arrows spent, the mage flung his first spear at Selam at the same moment Melanie completed her incantation. Clenching her fist in time with the final word, she felt the wolfsbane and copper grind together as the final syllable left her lips. A puff of smoke announced the components' destruction and Melanie stumbled forward as the force that had been pinning her to the wall abruptly disappeared.

She immediately began a new incantation, reaching into to her cloak for components.

The brigand mage recoiled as though smacked and the spear that had been heading toward Selam veered off course, sailing far away from the swordsman. Eyes wide in sudden fright, the mage screamed, "BITCH!" and made a pushing gesture with both hands.

The spear, which had been hanging in the air pointing at Selam, turned and streaked toward Melanie. Her incantation forgotten as her throat clenched, she found herself frozen in place, unable to move as she watched death approach. She could not even manage a scream.

An unexpected blow from the side sent her tumbling to the ground, a heavy weight upon her.

Selam grunted at the impact as well, his eyes going wide for a moment. Then he rolled off her. She gasped as she saw the spear protruding from his side. His breath came in short, rasping pants and he clutched at the shaft of the spear.

Melanie had no chance to assist him though. A great force took hold of her by the throat again and lifted her to her feet. The mage! She tried to begin her incantation again, but when she opened her mouth, the force pinned her arms to her sides and forced her jaws apart.

Sparing only the briefest of glances at Selam, the brigand mage stalked toward her. "No one left to save you now, girl," he said.

Looking over his shoulder, Melanie saw Julian stirring. Though she was relieved to see him alive, he was obviously not going to be useful any time soon. Over to the right, Raedrick and Farzal remained locked in their duel. Both men now bled from wounds: Raedrick on his left upper arm, Farzal on his right hip. But neither seemed to notice what was happening with her.

Melanie looked around frantically. Where was everyone else? Surely one of the archers, or some of the other townsfolk, would come.

But there was no one else. The mage was right. She was on her own, and helpless.

"You will tell me who betrayed our secrets to you," said the mage. Standing directly in front of her, his breath was hot on her face and unpleasant. She instinctively tried to recoil, but was held fast by the force of his spell. "Tell me sooner, and you will suffer less. Delay?" His lips twisted into a sneer and he looked her up and down. Then he licked his lips, and Melanie had no doubt what he intended to do to her.

The mage traced the edge of her jaw with his index finger. Helpless to move away, Melanie cringed inwardly and tried to think of a way to escape. If she could only move her arms, the knife she kept up her right sleeve could...

Unexpectedly, the force holding her jaws apart disappeared. Shutting her mouth quickly, she moved her jaw from side to side, feeling grateful in spite of herself at the relief.

"Talk, girl. Let's end this quickly."

Melanie swallowed the saliva that had been pooling in her mouth and cleared her throat. "He's dead," she replied. It was the simple truth, but she knew it would get her nowhere.

The mage sniffed. "Don't take me for a fool."

Melanie glanced over his shoulder and her spirits buoyed to see Farzal fall, hamstrung by a low cut from Raedrick's saber. "Your boss is about to die."

The mage's eyes widened and he looked back at the dueling men. Raedrick stepped toward the fallen Farzal and raised his saber for the killing blow. The mage cursed and extended a grasping hand toward him, and Raedrick froze in place.

Raedrick's eyes widened in surprise and he glanced around. Seeing the mage and Melanie, his face dropped in recognition of what was happening. On the ground before him, Farzal went from cringing in anticipation of Raedrick's blow to grinning in victory.

Melanie's spirits, so recently buoyed, sank like a stone. A sob welled up, and though she tried to suppress it she nevertheless felt tears stream down her cheeks. It was not until she wiped the tears away that she realized that her arms were free.

The brigand mage must have decided she was incapable of doing him harm; as close as he was, he could stop any incantation she tried well before it could be completed. The fool disregarded what she could do with her hands when he used the energy he needed to trap her arms to trap Raedrick instead. Knowing with certainty that he never would have disregarded a man so, Melanie felt more than a little satisfaction as she shook the knife from its sheath in her sleeve into her right hand and plunged it into the side of the mage's neck.

Chapter Twenty-Nine

Paying Tribute

Isenholf rose to a sitting position. He clutched at his wounded leg with his left hand, but grabbed his sword from the ground with his right. Looking up at Raedrick with a cruelly triumphant grin, he said, "You should have taken my offer."

Raedrick strained against the force holding him fast. They had come so close! He had long since stopped believing in fairness, but all the same the injustice of losing this way was too much to take.

Isenholf pushed himself across the ground using his good foot and drew his sword back. "Time to die," he said as he thrust upward with his blade.

All at once, the force holding Raedrick vanished, and he brought his saber down. The two blades met in the air before his belly, but not before Isenholf's sword tip struck home. For a heartbeat, he felt his mail straining and he knew it was going to fail. Then he twisted his hips and leaned backward. The sword cut a trail upward from his navel up to the lower ribs on his left side before the impact of his saber forced it aside. The pain of the wound told him his mail had failed at least partially. But it was not the crushing agony of a death blow, so he counted his blessings.

Isenholf's eyes went wide with shock at Raedrick's sudden movement. He lost his grip on his sword as Raedrick's saber struck it, and he collapsed back onto the ground. "How?" he said weakly.

Raedrick glanced over to the side and saw the mage lying on the ground, blood spurting from a wound in his neck, and Melanie helping Julian to his feet. "You chose your friends poorly," he said. Turning back to Isenholf, he moved the edge of his saber to the side of the brigand's neck.

"Do it," Isenholf said through gritted teeth.

He almost did. But looking down at the brigand, helpless on the ground, he recalled the screams of the villagers that day, the day he decided to follow Isenholf's earlier lead and desert. A very different reason, but the same path. If he killed Isenholf now, while he was helpless, how would he be better than what he had run from?

Raedrick shook his head and stepped back a pace. "No."

Isenholf looked at him with unbelieving eyes. He opened his mouth, but Raedrick cut him off with a boot to the nose. He fell back onto the ground, knocked senseless.

"See you at your trial."

With that, Raedrick turned away from the defeated brigand and hurried over to Melanie and Julian.

* * * * *

Julian was on his feet and standing next to Melanie by the

time Raedrick got to them. But while she stared at Selam as though stricken, he looked over the battlefield. Several of Isenholf's surviving men had already fled, those who were able to ride quickly outdistancing the others. There were not that many of them, maybe a dozen total. He had to hand it to Raedrick, the gambit with the archers worked beautifully.

Truth to tell, he was amazed they were still alive. Although from the look of things Selam would not be able to claim that for much longer.

Raedrick nodded to Julian in the same businesslike manner he always affected after a battle then squeezed Melanie's shoulder briefly before squatting down next to Selam.

"Did we…?" Selam said weakly.

Raedrick nodded. "Victory is ours."

Selam smiled. His cheeks were very pale and his breath came in shallow rattles. He reached with a trembling hand for his sword, lying off to the side just out of reach. Raedrick stretched out and moved the sword closer, placing the grip into the palm of Selam's hand. The dying man inhaled deeply and pressed the sword hilt to the center of his chest, over his heart.

"I have…" A sudden fit of coughing interrupted Selam's speech. "I have no sons," he said finally. "No one to pass it on to." He inhaled quickly and pressed the sword handle up to Raedrick's hands. "Use it with honor."

Raedrick's eyes widened and he shook his head. Pushing the sword back down to Selam, he replied, "Selam, I can't take…"

"Do not dishonor me." Another fit of coughing racked the stricken swordsman. His strength was fading quickly, but he managed to push the sword back up to Raedrick.

Julian's friend hesitated, then nodded slowly. His hands closed over Selam's on the hilt of his sword, and for a moment the two men looked at each other in silence. Then Selam smiled again and he let out a long rasping breath. His eyes glazed over and he did not breathe again.

Standing next to Julian, Melanie sobbed softly.

* * * * *

The funerals took place the next day. By tradition of the Vale, family and close friends of the fallen cleaned the bodies and dressed them in their Holiday best. Then, at first light, they carried the bodies down to the docks and laid them in dinghies made for just such an occasion. For the rest of the morning, acquaintances would come by to pay their respects and offer gifts for the fallen to use in the next life.

Constable Malory drew a visit from just about every person in town. Selam, much fewer. Perhaps it was because he was a transplant and liked to keep to himself. Regardless, as Julian stood next to the dinghies all morning and watched the relative paucity of visitors who came for him, irritation grew within in, eventually turning to anger. Friendly or not, Selam had given his life for the people of the Vale. He deserved more recognition than this.

By the time Melanie limped down to pay her respects, Julian was about ready to hit someone. But for some reason, seeing her there, even as bruised and battered as she was, made him feel better. She waited in line to offer flowers to Constable Malory and say a short prayer, but she did not linger. Until she came to Selam's dinghy.

Melanie nodded a greeting to Julian and moved quickly to the dinghy. She crouched down next to it and dropped something inside. When she did not rise after a few minutes, Julian became concerned and stepped over next to her. Crouching down as well, he saw that she was weeping.

They crouched there in silence for several minutes; Julian because he did not know what to say and did not want to intrude on her thoughts, Melanie for her own reasons. It was she who broke the silence.

"I only spoke with him once, and I was a condescending ass."

Julian was tempted to inquire how that was different from any other conversation she had, but thought better of it. That would have been perhaps a bit too harsh under the circumstances. Instead, he reached out and gave her shoulder a gentle squeeze.

"I didn't know him well, but he was a man of honor. Protecting you was his duty, so he did the right thing."

She nodded. "I know. That's what makes it so hard."

Julian drew a deep breath. "I've been fuming all morning about how many more people have been paying respects to Malory than him. Why was he so less deserving than Malory, you know? He deserves just as much a tribute from these people, and they're snubbing him. But now I think maybe that's ok. The fact that you're alive and able to carry on, that's a better tribute than some trinkets thrown into a boat."

Melanie nodded slowly, but didn't say anything. She just reached up, laid her hand atop his, and squeezed it gently.

* * * * *

At noon, the official funeral procession, consisting of the Mayor, Lydelton's High Priest, and the deceased's families, followed by musicians playing a memorial dirge on pipes and harps, walked from the Temple down to the docks.

The usual funeral ingredients came next: selected stories from the person's life, words of encouragement for the mourning, reminders to hope in the Gods and look forward to righteousness' rewards in the next life. Julian listened impassively, paying little heed to those words, meaningless as they were. Melanie and Raedrick stood at his side. She wept again. He stood at attention as if he was still in the Army, which Julian supposed was appropriate.

After all the words had been said, men hoisted sails on the dinghies, untied the boats from the dock, and pushed them out into the lake. The light breeze filled the dinghies' sails, carrying them further from shore. When they were about fifty yards out, Hiram and Rolf, carrying bows, limped to the end of the dock along with Gilroy, who carried a lit torch. The bowmen nocked and held their arrow tips into the torch's flame. Tips afire, the men drew back and sighted in carefully.

The loosed arrows rose in a graceful arc then descended, landing squarely in the center of each dinghy. Flammable materials had been strategically placed in each, and when the arrows struck the flames quickly spread until both dinghies were aflame from bow to stern.

The crowd gradually filtered away until only the deceased's closest family and friends remained. Julian, Raedrick, and Melanie remained even after they had departed, only leaving when the last remnants of the dinghies had sunk beneath the water of the lake.

Chapter Thirty

Home By The Lake

The next morning, a knock on their door took Julian and Raedrick by surprise.

"You weren't expecting any visitors, were you?" asked Raedrick.

Julian shook his head with a shrug, then walked over to the door and pulled it open. Mayor Brimly stood outside in the hallway.

"I hope I am not interrupting, gentlemen. May I come in?"

"Please," replied Julian as he opened the door fully and stepped out of Mayor Brimly's way.

He walked across the room to the window. Looking outside, he spoke as though talking to the town outside.

"You gentlemen did the people of this town a great service." Turning back to face them, he smiled apologetically.

"I know our agreement was that I would not act on my knowledge of your desertion from the Army if you helped us. That I would let you go about your lives as you see fit."

Where was he going with this? Julian began to get a twinge of apprehension in the pit of his stomach.

Mayor Brimly continued, "But I have a better idea."

Raedrick replied in a tight, angry tone. "If you're thinking of reneging on the deal..."

Mayor Brimly raised his hands in a placating manner. "Not at all. Not at all. I just thought maybe you would prefer an alternative."

"What alternative?"

"Malory is dead. Fendig..." The Mayor scowled and muttered a curse under his breath. Then, giving them a direct, serious look, he went on. "This town could use a couple good men to take their places. Frankly, I can't think of anyone more qualified than the two of you."

That was not what Julian expected to hear. He and Raedrick? Constables? The thought was so ludicrous that he almost burst out laughing. Only the Mayor's serious tone and demeanor stopped him.

"How are you going to explain to the kingdom your putting two deserters on the town payroll as law enforcement?" he asked, in lieu of laughter. "Because they *will* ask, you know."

Raedrick nodded in agreement. "We appreciate the offer, but it's too much of a risk..."

The Mayor snorted loudly. "The blasted kingdom's near enough forgotten us up here. Most all the major trade goes through the southern passes these days, so we're hardly worth noticing most times. We haven't even seen a tax collector in five years." He chuckled in amusement and shook his head. "That's got some in town asking why I bother collecting the taxes at all. They say I should just give the money back."

"Why don't you?"

The Mayor looked at Julian as though he was daft. "I'm not a fool, am I? Some day the kingdom will remember to send a tax collector, and he'll want every penny. Better to have the money set aside."

"You make our point for us," Raedrick said. "They will return, and you'll have to answer questions."

The Mayor made a dismissive gesture. "The Gods alone know how long it will be before that happens. And we can deal with it then if it does. In the meantime, you could have a good life here. And you'd be doing us a service, too. Who knows, when the kingdom does think to come calling, could be your serving here would be grounds enough to forgive your other offenses." He raised his one eyebrow. "Can't hurt, that's for sure. Think you'll get a better deal somewhere else?"

Julian had to admit, Brimly made a good argument. And truth be told, their plan had always been a bit nebulous beyond putting as much distance as possible between themselves and the war zone. It was true, though. They were much more likely to be caught and hanged near a large city than in a fly-speck of a town in the middle of nowhere. He half-smiled at those words, which both he and Melanie used not so long ago. He had to admit this place had grown on him.

"What do you think?" Julian turned to see Raedrick looking thoughtfully at him. From the expression on his face, Julian could tell he was mostly sold on the concept.

"I guess it wouldn't be too horrible to stay here for a while longer." He grinned and clapped Raedrick on the shoulder. "You get to be the Deputy, though."

Raedrick rolled his eyes but returned Julian's grin. Turning back to the Mayor, he held out his hand. "It looks like you have a deal, Mr. Mayor."

The Mayor took Raedrick's hand and shook it, then shook Julian's as well. "I'm glad to hear it. Welcome home, gentlemen."

Welcome home. Julian liked the sound of that.

* * * * *

Julian knocked on Melanie's door with his usual staccato rhythm. She took her time in answering. Naturally. When the door finally swung open, she wore a severe expression, as though she was prepared to lash whomever it was that had disturbed her up one side and down the other. Seeing him, her scowl faded, replaced by something that almost, but not quite, resembled a smile.

"Good afternoon, Melanie," Julian said with a jaunty grin.

She sniffed and turned away, retreating into her sitting room. She left the door open, though, so he took it upon himself to follow her inside.

"How are you holding up?"

Melanie shrugged and settled down on her couch. Sitting on the coffee table was a small figurine of a woman carved from a black substance of some sort. Julian thought it might be coal, but it reflected the light from her window slightly. What was it?

Noting his gaze, Melanie touched the figurine with her index finger. "I found this among Farzal's mage's belongings," she said. "Have you ever seen obsidian?"

He shook his head.

"It is made when the molten rock from a volcano cools." She looked back at him and rolled her eyes in consternation as she saw the confusion on his face. "Don't tell me you've never heard of a volcano."

He shook his head again.

"A mountain that releases smoke and spews out fire?"

Well why did she not say that in the first place? He said as much, and she chuckled.

"Julian, you amaze me sometimes." She patted the figurine again. "Anyway, I believe this is the object that controls the trans-planar rift in the hills. I have no idea how it works, though."

"I'm sure you'll figure it out in time." He paused for a moment before adding, "I have some news."

"Oh?"

Julian grinned and reached into his pocket. As he withdrew his new badge of office, the silver fist holding the dangling scales of justice, Melanie's eyes widened.

"You've got to be joking. Raedrick as well?"

He nodded.

She shook her head and stood up, then made a little curtsy in his direction. "It seems these yokels truly are desperate. Congratulations. I think."

Julian smirked in amusement. Leave it to her to ensure even a compliment held a little barb. Strangely enough, he found he did not mind. "Raedrick and I were hoping you would remain here as well."

Melanie snorted. "Why on earth would I want to do that? This place is…"

"Not nearly as bad as you've been saying, and you know it."

She was silent for a long moment while she sat back down again. Finally she nodded. "Fine, I'll admit there is a certain rustic charm here. That doesn't answer why I should stay."

"Did you have a destination in mind when you signed on with that caravan or were you just putting miles behind you?"

Melanie stiffened, looking at him through narrowed eyes.

"I don't know what you left behind, and it really doesn't matter. You could work your craft here and no one will get in your way. Hell," he gestured toward the window, "most folks think you're even more of a hero than me."

"That's not particularly hard to believe."

At least she grinned slightly when she said that. Julian could not help but chuckle and nod in response. "Well think about it at least. I don't doubt we'll need to contract for your help from time to time, and I've already heard a number of people talking about how useful it will be to have a professional mage in town." He stood up. "Isenholf was right about one thing. If a person needs to hide, there are far worse places than here, but few better."

With that, he walked over to the door.

"Julian."

He stopped and looked back at her over his shoulder.

"It has been a long time since I've been made to feel welcome anywhere," she said, "or since I've had anyone I can call a friend." She drew in a long breath and looked at him. He was shocked to see that she wore an expression of gratitude. "Thank you. I will seriously consider your offer."

Julian nodded and left. She was going to stay, he could see it in her eyes.

As he descended the stairs toward the Taproom, he passed one of the inn's cleaning maids, who stopped and made a quick curtsy. "Constable," she said respectfully, by way of greeting.

Julian blinked, surprised for a heartbeat. Then he smiled and replied, "Good afternoon," before continuing on his way.

He could feel her eyes on his back as he walked away, as well as the respect, awe almost, contained in her gaze. The reality of his new position hit him, and he shook his head in wonder. He was a respected public figure. Who would have thought?

An Excerpt from

Out-Dweller, Glimmer Vale Chronicles #2

Now available from Michael Kingswood and SSN Storytelling

Chapter One

Fresh Kill

Baelin unstrung his bow and shoved it over his right shoulder, under the strap of his backpack, then crouched down and gathered the spoils of the day's hunt. It had taken a while to dress out the buck and he would lose the light soon; it was well past time to get back home. Ilsa would begin to worry if he tarried too much longer, to say nothing of the scolding she would unleash if he caused dinner to grow cold.

He smiled at the contradiction in her possible reactions - and he had seen them both before. But then that was the essence of woman was it not? Contradiction.

The buck was heavier than it looked, and it took a moment to get it settled over his left shoulder and balanced well. Baelin adjusted his brown hunting cloak a bit so that it settled better over himself; summer was coming to a close, and the evening's chill had grown bitter over the last week. Then he set off down the hill toward town.

The northern slopes of the mountains surrounding Glimmer Vale were covered in dense evergreens and he had to weave his way through a seeming maze of tree trunks as he made his way back toward Lake Glimmermere and Lydelton. Many a man with limited experience had gotten lost in these woods, called the Glamorwood by the locals. Some of the more gullible townsfolk told tall tales of spirits living amongst the trees. So with the exception of logging expeditions that never went in further than the edges of the forest and outdoorsmen like Baelin, most people from Lydelton and the town's surrounds did not venture here.

Which suited Bealin just fine. Most people were not worth dealing with, and the fewer who came here the more likely he was to be able to enjoy the woods in peace.

And it made venison more rare in town, which meant he could charge more for his take.

Baelin's smile grew a bit more broad at that thought.

The shadows were growing long now as the sun made its way to its resting place in the east, below the ridges of the Saddleback Mountains. Off to the right, a Night Thrush called out, breaking the silence with its ululating chirp. Baelin quirked an eyebrow; it was a bit early to hear that particular breed up and about, but the early bird gets the worm, or something.

He descended further, moving carefully to avoid tripping in the elongating shadows. After about a quarter of an hour he stopped for a moment. The buck was heavy. That was good, made for more meat. But it was growing uncomfortable carrying it as he was; the muscles in his left shoulder were beginning to shout in protest and he felt a cramp coming on.

Grumbling to himself, Baelin rolled his right shoulder and shoved the bow further down. Then with a huff he shifted the buck over to his right and rebalanced himself before heading off again.

A few paces later, a snort from off to his left stopped

Baelin in his tracks. What was that?

He turned his head, peering around carefully and trying to ignore the sudden whisper of alarm that began to take shape within him. He had never heard a sound like that out here before, and he had tracked or hunted just about everything that lived in these woods at one time or another.

The snort came again, a bit louder this time. With it came a strange odor that seeped into the normal scent of fallen pine needles like a bit of dye dropped into a cup of water. He almost had not noticed it was there at all, subtle as the new scent was. Sharp and tangy, with an unpleasant undertone, like something rotten.

Baelin scowled, that whisper becoming more like a person speaking in a normal tone of voice now. He shivered from a surge of adrenalin. Something was not right here.

He stood there for a long several moments, his free left hand resting on the grip of his long hunting knife, where it was sheathed on his hip. His left was not his best hand, but he was not completely inept with it. And right then the feel of the weapon in hand was all that mattered.

The odor grew stronger, and a branch snapped somewhere behind him. Baelin turned quickly. The buck slid off his shoulder and landed on the ground with a muffled thud, but he paid it no mind.

He squinted, trying to see what was out there, but the light was going fast, and here beneath the canopy of the trees it was already getting on toward twilight.

He saw nothing, but that was no comfort. *Something* was out there. Something foul.

Calm down. You're not some tenderfoot, out in the woods for the first time and scared of his own shadow. It's just a hog.

The thought was logical, but Baelin's instincts rejected it out of hand. No hog ever smelled like this.

He looked around for another minute or so, the strange odor growing steadily stronger the entire while, but still saw nothing. Neither was there any other sound besides the tree limbs stirring in the breeze and the pounding of his own heart.

It was nothing. He just stumbled a bit too close to the remains of some predator's kill.

And speaking of which, he had his own kill to take care of, and it was well past too late to be out in these woods.

Baelin crouched back down and maneuvered the buck back onto his shoulder - his left this time. Straightening, he turned back toward town.

And came face to face with something right out of his nightmares.

His scream, loud and terrified, echoed through the woods for a long several seconds before it abruptly cut off in a strangled gurgle.

Then all was silent.